HALLOWEEN AT THE HAUNTED HOUSE

A MADDIE MILLS COZY MYSTERY
BOOK FIVE

CINDY BELL

ISBN: 9798861253062

CHAPTER 1

Maddie Mills squeezed the thin, black leg of the candy spider between her fingertips and hovered the cupcake topper over the bright orange frosting piled on the vanilla cupcake.

She lowered it onto the large cupcake. Its long legs draped across the center and stretched to the edge of the frosting.

"Perfect." She clapped her hands, then took a step back as she looked over the rows of cupcakes lined up on the large, metal table before her. "Great, only about a thousand more to go."

"Don't worry, Aunt Maddie, we're going to get them done." Katie's youthful optimism gave her voice a cheerful bounce.

"Yes, we will." Maddie flashed a smile in her niece's direction. "I'm so glad I have your help. How are the pumpkins going?"

"So far, so good. I love the way the orange color stands out against the green frosting. It's hard to resist taking a bite myself." Katie laughed as she ducked away from the warning glare her aunt sent in her direction. "I know, I know, no sampling the goods when we're so close to our deadline."

"It's a crazy rush to get so many treats ready for only one night of the year." Maddie began to add a spider to the top of another cupcake. "It's fun, even though it's quite a rush."

"Yes, but it's almost over. Once we get these cupcakes delivered, that's it, right? We can go off and enjoy our own Halloween festivities. Did you get a costume?" Katie added a pumpkin to a cupcake.

"Oh no, I'm not really into those kinds of things. At my age, it's just fun to hand out candy." Maddie stretched her neck back and groaned. As she neared the end of her forties, her body had begun protesting in new and inventive ways. "This is rather intense. I haven't stopped all day. I think I might need to take a break and visit the dogs."

"Go for it. I'm sure they'll be so happy to see

you. I'll keep going, so I can have a break when you come back." Katie picked up another bag of candy pumpkins. "These might be a lot of work, but they're turning out so spectacular, the customers are going to love them."

"Let's hope so." Maddie did her best to infuse her voice with as much enthusiasm as Katie seemed to have in abundant supply. She yearned for those years, the twenties, when everything felt unpredictable but also possible.

As Maddie opened the door to the backyard behind the bakery, her two dogs bounded toward her. She managed to pull the door shut before they could slip past.

"No way. No dogs allowed inside." Maddie grinned as she dropped into a crouch to greet the West Highland White Terriers. "But I can come out here and play with you, can't I?" She grabbed one of their toys and tossed it across the yard. "Get it, Polly. Here's one for you, Bella." She threw another toy, then squinted up at the sunny sky. Despite the fall season, the temperature had reached an unusual high.

She smiled as Polly and Bella each brought their toys back for her to toss again. She flung them both, then stood up.

"Oh, my goodness!" A woman in a long, green skirt, paired with an orange top jumped back from the fence she'd just walked up to. She pressed her hand against her chest and laughed. "You startled me, Maddie. I didn't see you there."

"I'm sorry, Amber." Maddie grinned at her best childhood friend, Amber West, who had quickly become her best friend again after Maddie had moved back to her hometown. "But it's a nice surprise, right?"

"Yes, very nice, and I have a nice surprise for you, too." Amber's bright eyes sparkled as she settled them on Maddie's. "You're going to love me."

"I already do. Out with it."

"I scored you a great gig. Well, my mother did, but I told her I'd tell you. She overheard that someone was looking for catering for a group tonight, specifically cupcakes. Of course, my mother made sure she got the name and made all of the arrangements. So, all you have to do is call this number and get the order." Amber handed her a slip of paper.

"Oh, that's wonderful." Maddie took the paper and stared at the phone number. "Wait, did you say tonight?"

"Yes, tonight." Pride filled Amber's voice. "I just know my mother was bragging about you."

"But, Amber, I'm in the middle of finishing off the orders for tonight, including a big one. I'm not sure I can fill this in time." Maddie chewed on her bottom lip for a moment. "I really appreciate the offer, but I don't think it's going to work out."

"Wait, you haven't heard the best part." Amber walked closer to the fence. "It's at Becket House."

"No." Maddie almost dropped the slip of paper. "Are you serious?"

"Yes, dead serious." Amber laughed. "Is that a bad joke?"

"I haven't been anywhere near that house in decades. I thought it would have collapsed by now. It's really still around?" Maddie recalled the three-story monstrosity that featured large windows with arches curved on the top of them. It was the most frightening house she'd ever set eyes on.

"It is. A young couple is running it now. Dirk and Cynthia. Dirk is the old owners' grandson, and Cynthia is his new wife. It's still operating as a haunted B&B. The owners have always done all kinds of special events. Tonight they're having a show filmed there about the house, and they have some guests staying for Halloween, so at the last minute they decided they wanted some cupcakes. Are you sure you can't do it?" A hint of a whine entered Amber's voice as she continued. "I was really hoping I could go with you because I'd love to see the inside of that place. Do you remember when we chickened out that night?"

"Oh, do I!" Maddie laughed. "I think it was way worse than chickening out. We ran so fast, I almost fell on my face. I never wanted to go back there."

"Right, but that's when we were kids. Now we know better, and we can get an inside view. Plus, I'm sure they'll mention your bakery on the show if we play our cards right." Amber leaned closer to the fence. "What do you say? I can help with anything you need, and I'm sure your sister will, too."

Maddie shivered as a memory from many years before played through her mind. The legend about the house was that it was haunted by the Becket bride. Maddie had heard so many stories about the house before going there that she had actually thought she had seen the ghost of the bride in the attic window. She hadn't erased a single detail about that moment.

Every instinct warned Maddie not to go there again. But maybe that was why she had to say yes. Why let herself be scared over something so silly? It must have just been her overactive imagination. It would be a fun evening with her friend and a great boost for her still fledgling business. Seeing the excitement in Amber's eyes stirred some excitement of her own.

"Sure. Why not? You're right. It would be great for the business. But I'm definitely going to need your help."

"I'll call my mom to help, too. It'll be so much fun." Amber continued toward the front of the bakery while Maddie stepped back inside through the back door.

"Katie, I think I might have gotten us into some big trouble!" Maddie called out.

CHAPTER 2

"*D*on't worry, Maddie, the troops have arrived!" Tammy Webber made a trumpeting noise as she walked into the bakery with Iris West just behind her. "We're ready to make some pastries."

Maddie breathed a sigh of relief at the sight of her younger sister and Amber's mother.

"Or cupcakes. Whatever you need." Iris grinned as she joined them in the kitchen.

"Both. We need help with both." Maddie paused long enough to place a light peck on Iris' cheek. "Thank you so much for getting me this job. I just hope we can get it done on time. We still have to finish the other orders for today."

"No problem. Just put us to work." Iris rolled up her flowy sleeves until they were up near her shoulders.

Within a few minutes, Maddie had arranged an assembly line for the cupcakes. Halloween music blasted through the speakers in the bakery, but it could barely be heard over the laughter and conversation that filled the large space.

"So, we're all going, right?" Katie filled a box with cupcakes. "I'm so excited to see the place. I've never been anywhere haunted before."

"Yup, we're going to make it a girls' trip. It might be a short one, but it will be fun." Maddie smiled.

"It's not really haunted, Katie." Iris waved her hand dismissively.

"Oh, don't tell that to Maddie." Amber smiled as she glanced over at her.

"It was nothing. It was just my active imagination." Maddie laughed.

"Oh, I remember that night when you two came running home." Tammy finished adding vanilla buttercream to a cupcake.

"Running home from where?" A familiar voice floated into the back of the bakery from the dining area. "Maddie, are you busy?" Jake Holden stuck his head into the kitchen and chuckled. "Well, yes, it looks like you are."

It still shocked Maddie to see the skinny boy, who used to pester her all the time, all grown up and wearing a uniform. He wasn't just a police officer but the chief of police, and you couldn't describe him as skinny anymore. His muscular frame, piercing green eyes, and confident smile all worked together to distract her.

"Jake, come in. Grab an apron. You can help." Amber waved him toward the cupcakes.

"Sorry, I'm afraid I can't." Jake gestured to the badge he wore on his chest. "I'm on double duty today with all the crazy things that can happen on Halloween. I just stopped by because I had hoped to grab a cup of coffee with you later, Maddie. What do you think?"

"I'm sorry, I can't. We have a lot of orders we still need to finish, and Iris and Amber got me this great gig catering an event tonight, and as long as we stay on track, we should be ready for it. But it's out on Bay Point, so I probably won't be back until late." Maddie continued piping frosting on what she hoped was the last of the cinnamon cupcakes for the order. She had to do a recount to make sure.

"Out on Bay Point?" Curiosity narrowed Jake's

eyes. "But the only thing out there is Becket House."

"Yes, that's it." Amber grinned. "We're going to be in an actual haunted house on Halloween."

"It's not haunted." Iris put her hands on her hips.

"We'll find out tonight, I guess." Katie grinned.

"No, that's not happening." Jake's tone hardened.

Maddie froze in the middle of her count and looked up at him. "Excuse me? Are you telling us we can't go to Bay Point?"

Tammy shifted closer to Maddie in a protective gesture.

"It's not safe out there. And there's a storm coming in." Jake shook his head. "Call and cancel."

"What?" Maddie's mind spun as she tried to piece together how he thought he could speak to her that way. "I will not cancel. I've already made all of these cupcakes. That would cause me a loss. Besides, the storm isn't due to come in until the morning, if it even comes this way. It's still sunny out. There isn't a cloud in the sky."

"Maddie, I don't want to argue about this. I don't want you out there, not on Halloween or any other night." Jake's stern tone silenced everyone in the kitchen.

"Oh." Maddie studied the tension in his expression and the way he squared his shoulders. "You're scared, aren't you? You believe it's haunted, too?" The thought surprised her. Jake never indicated he believed in anything paranormal.

"I didn't say that," Jake snapped his words. "Just take my advice for once, okay?"

"Like I said, I already took the order. I'm not scared of any ghosts." Maddie gave a short laugh and tried to return to her count.

"Something isn't right about that place. I've been trying to figure it out for years. It isn't about it being haunted." Jake pulled his hat off and gripped it tight in his hands. "Do I really have to beg you not to go?"

"You can do whatever you please." Maddie looked into his eyes. "It's not going to change anything. I've made a commitment, and I have to honor it. The reputation of the bakery would take a huge hit if I didn't."

"Then I'll go with you." Jake reached for the radio on his belt.

"No, you won't. You need to stay here in case

the kids decide to go wild or the parties spill out into the streets. You just have to relax. I'm not going alone. We're all going. We're just going to deliver the order and leave. I'll call you to let you know when I'm back in town, and if it's not too late, and you're free, we'll get that cup of coffee. All right?" Maddie held her breath as she wondered if he would push it.

"I guess I don't have a choice." Jake turned away from her. "Call me as soon as you're back." He glanced back over his shoulder at the group of women. "And all of you, be careful, please."

"We'll be fine, Jake." Iris swept her hands through the air and smiled. "If there's anything spooky going on, I'll be able to handle it." She laughed.

"Just be careful." Jake turned and left the bakery.

Maddie watched him go. Almost immediately, the chatter and laughter returned. But Maddie's smile didn't spread quite as wide. She'd learned a lot about Jake since she'd come back to town. It had surprised her to discover that his annoying habit of telling her what to do ever since they were kids was about keeping her safe, not bossing her around.

Still, she didn't like that he seemed to think he could tell her what to do, but something about his tone and expression made her wonder, if it wasn't the ghosts he was worried about, what had him spooked?

CHAPTER 3

ammy helped load the last box of cupcakes onto the back seat of Maddie's SUV. Maddie had just finished the large cupcake delivery, and now the rush to get to Bay Point had begun.

"Don't let Jake get to you, Maddie. Halloween can be a busy time for the police. People are always acting a little wild. He's just a bit wound up." Tammy closed the door to the back seat of the car. "We're going to have a great time."

"I don't know how great it's going to be if we don't get moving." Maddie squinted up at the sky as dark clouds rolled across the sunset. "It looks like the rain is coming earlier than we expected."

"Then we'd better get going." Tammy smiled.

"You and Amber drive ahead with the cupcakes. The rest of us, and the dogs, will be right behind you."

"Are you sure you don't mind taking them? With the bad weather, I'd hate to leave them at home, and there isn't really time to take them home at this point." Maddie sat in the driver's seat.

"It's no trouble at all. Katie will keep them entertained. I'll send Amber right out." Tammy turned toward the bakery.

Maddie started her car, then closed her eyes for a moment. It had been a whirlwind of a day. She hoped the delivery would go smoothly, and maybe things would be as fun as Tammy promised. She opened her eyes again to find heavy raindrops striking the windshield.

Amber pulled open the passenger door and slid inside. "It's getting nasty out, huh?" She buckled her seat belt. "I hope we can get to Bay Point before the real rain starts. It can get pretty impassable out there if it rains really hard."

"Maybe it's just a stray rain band." Maddie pulled out of the parking lot of the bakery and settled in for the thirty-minute drive. "The weather website said it wouldn't arrive until the morning."

"Ugh, you can't rely on that website. You have

to listen to the local newscaster. He's been predicting these storms for almost thirty years now, and he's always right." Amber cleared her throat as Maddie stepped on the gas. "I did a quick check on his website before we left, and it doesn't look good. We should definitely do the delivery and get back on the road right away."

"Because of the rain, or because of what we might see there?" Maddie shot her a quick look and a smile. "Don't worry, I'm not judging. You know what happened that night."

"No, I don't. You never told me." Amber gave her an eager smile. "Are you going to tell me now?"

"It's not important, really. You remember how curious we were about the house. We thought we were so brave, after hearing all the stories about the ghosts. But the truth is, I just didn't believe in any ghost stories. I didn't think there was anything to be afraid of, so I wasn't worried at all."

"But then the bird flew out of the trees. It scared us both because it was so large, and we both took off running." Amber laughed.

"Yes, but you were way ahead of me. When I looked back at the house, I saw this woman in the attic window. Although, I wouldn't even call her a woman. She didn't look real. Her skin was so white, and she had deep, dark circles under her eyes. She waved at me. I ran as fast as I could and never went back to that house."

"I'm not surprised."

"But it was stupid. It must have just been my imagination getting away from me after all the stories I'd heard about the Becket bride." Maddie looked in her rearview mirror to confirm that Tammy's car followed at a short distance behind her.

"It will be good to go out there again and actually see the place." Amber smiled as she looked over at Maddie. "So, tell me all about Chief Grumpypants. When is your next date planned for?"

"We haven't made plans, yet. Things keep getting in the way." Maddie stepped on the gas. "Let's just get this delivery made. I'm starting to get nervous about the weather."

"Or about the conversation?" Amber leaned her head back against the seat. "Why don't you want to talk about him?"

"It's not that I don't want to talk about him, it's just that I don't really know what to say." Maddie turned off the highway onto a short side road that led onto a long causeway. Already, the water lapped at the edges of the structure. "One minute, I think I might be ready for a relationship with him, and I'm so excited by it, the next, he talks to me the way he did today, and I have my doubts."

"Yes, it wasn't his best moment. But I think his intentions are good," Amber said.

"I know. I guess I'm still hesitant. It wasn't that long ago that I found out about all of my ex-husband's lies, and my life as I knew it vanished. Maybe things are just moving a little too fast with Jake. Maybe I need more time to get over my failed marriage first." Maddie squinted as the rain fell even harder. Her ex-husband had been gambling for years and left her with a huge debt that had lost them their house, which meant she had to move back to Bayview to live in her late parents' house. He had been arrested for fraud and was in jail. "It's not too far up ahead now." She glanced up at the rearview mirror and watched as Tammy made her way across the causeway. "I hope the bridge isn't under water by the time we leave."

Amber looked through the side mirror and made a sharp noise in her throat.

"That water is rising fast, Maddie." She glanced over at her. "I hate to say this, but Jake might have been right. There's a good chance we're not getting out of here tonight, no matter how fast we make this delivery."

"Great." Maddie's shoulders slumped as she predicted the "I told you so." "Should we turn around?"

"I think it's too late for that."

"Do you think they'll let us stay?" Maddie asked.

"I'm sure they will." Amber's cell phone began ringing. "It's Mom. I'll put it on speaker. Hello?" She set the phone on the console between them.

"Did you see how high the water is?" A tightness entered Iris' normally warm and relaxed voice. "It's rising fast. It already looks too high to turn back."

"Yes, we were just talking about it. It looks like we might have to camp out at the B&B for the night, unless the rain lets up." Maddie stared at the deluge of water that ran across the windshield. "Which I don't think it is."

"All right, I'll call ahead and let them know the situation. Sorry about this, Maddie. I guess it wasn't the best idea after all," Iris said.

"It's fine. No one could have predicted the storm coming this early or being so bad." Maddie rolled her eyes and mumbled her next words. "No one but

Chief Grumpypants." She slowed the car down to a rolling pace as the road in front of her disappeared under a steady flow of water. "At this point, we'll be lucky if we make it to the house."

Maddie continued down the road. The sight of the huge house ahead of her provided a sense of relief. She drove up the driveway, then looked in the rearview mirror and watched as Tammy's car pulled up behind hers.

Maddie looked around. The elevation of the driveway would keep them safe, for the moment, but the grounds surrounding the house were already pooling with water.

As she hopped out of her SUV, she noticed Iris opening an umbrella. But the whipping wind made it impossible to keep control of it.

"Oh, this is useless." Iris threw the umbrella back into Tammy's car.

Maddie walked over to the car. She peered through the window at the two pups running around the back seat and jumping across Katie's lap.

"They're so excited." Katie gathered them into her arms. "We all are. What a fun surprise to have a sleepover in a haunted house, right?" She grinned that impossibly positive grin.

Maddie's gaze swept up over the old house as

rain soaked through her clothes. With the backdrop of heavy clouds and a struggling sunset, it looked more eerie than ever. But the attic windows were dark, as were all the other windows, aside from the ones on the first story. The front door swung open and a man shouted to them.

"Get inside before the driveway turns into a mud pit!"

CHAPTER 4

"We have to get the cupcakes." Maddie started toward the back of her SUV.

"I'll get them, Aunt Maddie. You and Mom take the girls." Katie stepped out of the car into the river of water and handed Polly to Maddie and Bella to Tammy.

"I'll help." Amber followed Katie.

Maddie snuggled Polly close as she hurried toward the front door. Once inside, she greeted the man who had opened the door for her. He was tall and thin with an air of confidence.

"I'm Dirk." He gestured to a petite woman standing next to him. "This is my wife."

"Cynthia." She smiled.

"I'm Maddie." Maddie stepped aside and introduced Iris, Amber, Tammy, and Katie as they filed in. "Thank you so much for your order. Unfortunately, it looks like the weather took a sudden turn."

"Yes, it's all everyone is blustering about on the news. It took a hard right instead of the slow loop they were expecting. I'm just so glad you all got here in time. I was going to get the boat ready to go out and rescue you, just in case." Dirk looked at a man who walked into the room. He looked to be well into his seventies and was quite short and portly.

"Richard, it's good to see you." Iris walked over to him. "I didn't know you would be here tonight."

"Halloween is a special time, and we thought it would be nice to be here to help out if they need it." Richard gestured to Cynthia and Dirk.

A broad woman with a warm smile, who looked about the same age as Richard, walked into the entryway with a pile of thick towels.

"Here, dry yourselves off. There are some for the pups, too." She made kissing noises at the two dogs. "I'll get them a bowl of water as well."

Polly and Bella squirmed in Maddie's and Tammy's arms, eager to get down and make friends with the strangers.

"Hi, Barbara." Iris greeted the woman.

Barbara looked from the dogs to Iris.

"Oh, Iris. I'm so sorry you got caught up in this awful weather."

"Hopefully, it will clear up soon," Iris said.

"Let me take those for you, so you can get dried off." Dirk walked over to Katie and took the large, white box, then smiled as he inhaled deeply. "Oh, they smell amazing. These will definitely get us through the storm." He held out the box of cupcakes, so Amber could put hers on top.

"Is it as bad out there as they're saying?" A petite woman wearing socks, sweatpants, and a wrinkled T-shirt joined them in the entryway.

"Worse, I think." Barbara squinted through the window on the door. "But don't worry, we're safe here. This house has weathered many storms."

"We have plenty of rooms available for everyone to enjoy. Some of the guests haven't managed to make it before the storm. We'll just have to make the best of it." Cynthia smiled.

"I really appreciate you letting us stay here." Maddie held tight to the dogs' leashes. "These are my dogs, Polly and Bella. I promise they're well-behaved."

"Oh, I don't like little dogs." The woman in the

doorway scrunched up her nose as the dogs began to sniff her socks.

"Relax, Debbie. They're so cute. I'm sure they're just curious about you." A rumbling voice filled the air just before a muscular, handsome man, who was maybe in his late twenties or early thirties, joined them. "Wow, I had no idea the storm would be this bad. It will make for great background sounds. I'm going to make sure I get some recordings of the wind howling. Debbie, grab your sound stuff."

"Adam, if you think I'm going out in that weather, you're crazy." Debbie scowled at him.

"What am I paying you for?" Adam snapped back at her. "You'll do what I tell you to do."

"You don't own me." Debbie crossed her arms. "You can't force me to go out there."

"You were out there five minutes ago smoking, but you can't risk a little rain to get the audio we need? What kind of camerawoman are you? You're useless." Adam stormed past the grand stairway toward the entrance of the house.

A tall, willowy woman chased after him, calling out to him in a sweet, high-pitched voice. "Adam, don't be upset!"

"Leave me alone, Silla," Adam barked at her as he stormed off.

Maddie's attention was caught by the way the staircase loomed upward to the second story and farther to the third. She wanted to have a closer look.

"Don't mind them." Dirk rolled his eyes. "That's Silla, Adam's girlfriend. Adam is the producer, and Debbie is the camerawoman. They're always at each other's throats. They're supposed to be filming a documentary, but things have gone awry."

"Is that how you describe it?" Another man, thinner, with dark hair and big, brown eyes walked up to the group. "Because the way I see it, something criminal has taken place, and I don't care what Adam says about it, it can't be legal. You two really should have warned me about what he was up to."

"We decided not to get involved, Pierce." Cynthia looked him over. "We don't know how these things work. All we know is that you asked to film a documentary, and so did he."

"But I asked first, and you agreed to it." Pierce raised his voice.

"Calm down. We have enough to deal with right now. We have to make sure this house stays protected. If the bay floods, it might just get inside." Dirk glanced back at the others assembled in the doorway, finishing off drying their clothes and hair. "Just make yourselves comfortable. We're going to set a few of these up for a bit later and put the rest away." He held up the boxes. "And then get your rooms ready."

"We'll help set up the cupcakes," Maddie offered.

"Okay, thank you. But dry off first." Cynthia gestured to the towels. "We'll leave the cupcakes and a platter in the kitchen."

"Great." Maddie grabbed a towel.

Cynthia and Dirk walked out of the room.

"I told them not to do the show." Richard turned toward his wife.

"When do the kids ever listen to us?" Barbara waved her hand through the air.

"I'm going to check on a few things before the storm gets worse. I know this house inside and out. Barbara, will you help me?" Richard started toward the stairs.

"Right behind you, dear." Barbara followed him.

Pierce turned on his heel and walked off.

"Well, it looks like we've walked into quite a mess." Tammy bundled her towel up and stuck it under her arm. "But there are worse places to be marooned, I think." Her gaze wandered the opulent surroundings.

"You're right about that." Iris draped her arm over Amber's shoulders. "I had no idea it would be this beautiful inside."

"It's so dark, though." Katie peered up at the ceiling.

"They're probably playing up the idea of a haunted house," Amber said.

"Probably. I'm going to get the cupcakes organized." Maddie handed the dogs' leashes to Tammy.

"I'll help." Katie followed Maddie toward the kitchen.

"Wow, this is huge." Maddie looked around the kitchen.

"It is." Katie and Maddie walked over to the sink and washed their hands.

"We'll just set up a few for the moment." Maddie opened the cupcake box.

"These look great." Katie started filling the platter with cupcakes.

"We'll leave these for later." Maddie popped the lid back on the box.

"They can bring out the platter when they're

ready for them." Katie followed Maddie back toward the dining room.

"It's been a long drive and a lot of excitement for the dogs." Maddie walked over and took the leashes from Tammy. "I'm going to take them out before it gets any worse."

"I'll go with you." Tammy started to follow her toward the door.

"No, it's fine. You finish getting dry. I won't be long." Maddie opened the door and stepped back out into the whipping wind and rain.

CHAPTER 5

*a*s Maddie held tightly to the dogs' leashes to keep them close to her side, a figure approached, half-hidden by the heavy rain that continued to fall. She squinted and was able to identify the person as a woman.

"Have you seen Adam?" The woman walked toward her.

"No, I think he's out here somewhere making sound recordings." Maddie peered through the raindrops at the stunning face that looked back at her.

"I've been looking and I can't find him. If you see him, let him know Alexandra is looking for him, okay?"

"Sure, but I don't plan to be out here very long.

I'm Maddie. I came here to make a delivery, but the weather is so bad, I think we're all stuck now. You should get inside and warm up." Maddie looked over her rain-soaked clothes and the very thin body they covered. A good gust of wind might sweep her away.

"Yes, I'm going in now." Alexandra stepped past her and into the house.

"All right, girls, you need to do your thing, and fast, please." Maddie hunched her shoulders close to her cheeks and let the dogs nose their way through the puddles in search of a dry place to do their business. For once, she felt gratitude for the extra pounds she'd been fighting most of her adult life. The fierce winds that blew ruffled her sopping wet hair, and whipped at her raincoat and pants, but didn't knock her off-balance. She shielded her eyes from the sharp raindrops and let the dogs take the lead.

A few minutes later, she heard the unmistakable rush of water and felt a quick spark of panic. She hadn't been paying attention to where the dogs led her, and with her eyes shielded, she didn't notice they had neared the bay. The normally placid water churned and rushed forward, lapping over its usual boundaries in hard slaps and hungry stretches as it consumed more and more of what should have been dry land.

Maddie scooped up the dogs, who had thankfully finally relieved themselves, and scampered back away from the fluctuating edge. As she did, her gaze drifted over something unusual in the water. Her heart stopped at the sight of outstretched fingertips.

At first, Maddie felt the instinct to grab on, to help the person out of the water. But soon, she realized the fingers only moved in a beckoning motion because of the ebb and flow of the water. Her focus traveled along the open palm, across the arm, to a face that stared up at the tumultuous sky. His wide-open eyes didn't blink despite the relentless rain.

"Adam!" Maddie gasped his name as she recognized the man from when she'd first seen him only a short time before. Her exclamation of his name was quickly followed by her shriek that managed to overcome the rush of the wind.

"Hello?" Another voice carried to her from a short distance, though the rainfall and the darkness made it impossible to identify who it was. "Is someone hurt?"

"Help! Please!" Maddie held her dogs close in

her arms. With her adrenaline pumping, they felt light to her. A part of her couldn't believe the body in front of her was real, and another part wanted him to start laughing and declare it all some kind of Halloween prank.

"I'm coming. I see you." The voice grew close enough for Maddie to recognize it.

"Pierce?" Maddie squinted through the rain and saw him run toward her. "Pierce, it's Adam."

"What about him?" Pierce slowed down as he neared the edge of the water. "It's not safe for you to be so close to the water in this weather. You should take those dogs inside."

"It's Adam. He's dead. I think he drowned!" Maddie blurted out the words.

"What?" Pierce's gaze swung down to the water. He grabbed on to Maddie's shoulder and stumbled back a step.

Maddie willed her muscles to remain stable as his weight threatened to knock her off-balance, and her feet slid against the slick soil now flooded by several inches of water.

"Adam!" Pierce found his footing and leaned forward to grab hold of Adam's shoulders. He pulled the man out of the deeper water inch by inch. Pierce put his fingers against the side of Adam's neck. He looked up at Maddie and shook his head to confirm what she already knew. Adam didn't have a pulse.

"He must have slipped and been swept in." Maddie watched as the water swirled around in violent spurts and circles. "The way this walkway slants down, if a good rush of water caught him off guard, it could have happened."

"The way he drank makes it even more likely." Pierce pursed his lips as he looked down at the man he still grasped. "We'll have to get him out of the rain, or he might get swept away again."

A collection of voices called out from a short distance away. One voice shouted louder than all of them. "Maddie! Maddie, are you out there?"

Maddie recognized her sister's voice. She held tightly to the dogs as they wriggled in her grasp.

"Tammy, we're over here! Be careful!"

Tammy, Richard, and Amber emerged from the torrential rain.

"We heard a scream." Richard's voice held a tone of warning. "You shouldn't scream like that unless you're in trouble."

"She had a good reason." Pierce continued to slide Adam's body forward. "It looks like Adam hit the end of his good luck."

"Adam! Oh no!" Richard gasped.

"Let's get you inside." Amber stepped up to Maddie and Tammy.

"Wait, we have to get Adam inside. Someone take the dogs, so that I can help." Maddie put the dogs on the ground and handed Tammy their leashes.

"I'll help." Richard stepped forward.

"That's okay, Richard. I'll help." Amber clearly didn't want to risk the older man slipping.

"Be careful, Amber." Maddie sloshed through the water.

"What's going on?" Cynthia gasped as she walked up beside Richard, with Dirk following.

"Adam's dead." Richard pointed toward the body.

"Dead?" Dirk walked over to Pierce. "Let's get him inside."

"Give me his coat. It's weighing him down. It will be easier for you to carry him if he isn't wearing it." Cynthia held out her hands.

Dirk pulled off Adam's raincoat and handed it to Cynthia.

Maddie squeezed her eyes shut against the rain for a second, then opened them as they neared the house.

"What's wrong? Is everyone okay?" Katie stood in the doorway with a bright lantern in one hand. "Is that Adam?" She held the lantern out farther, then gasped. "Oh no! Did he drown?"

"It looks that way." Dirk tipped his head toward the door. "Can someone hold it open? We're going to have to carry him inside."

"Yes, I will." Katie held open the door.

Maddie caught sight of red marks around Adam's neck as the lantern light swept across his face. Her muscles tensed. It looked like the marks would turn into bruises. Drowning wouldn't cause marks like that, would it?

As they walked into the house, Maddie noticed Cynthia duck into a small room to hang Adam's raincoat on a hook by the door. She walked back out with a few towels in her hands and crossed the hall.

"Here, put him in the garage." Cynthia opened the door off to the side of the front hallway. "He should be okay in here until we can get someone to collect him."

She spread out two towels on the floor beside the car and they placed Adam's body on top of them.

"We can cover him with these." Cynthia handed the other two towels to Pierce. With Maddie's help he covered Adam's body with them. Cynthia looked up at the sound of footsteps above them. "What a terrible accident."

"We don't know for sure if it was an accident. All we know is he's dead," Maddie said.

"He drowned. What else could it be if not an accident?" Richard stared at her. "Are you trying to say you think he might have been murdered?"

CHAPTER 6

"*M*urdered?" A tall, slender woman stood in the garage doorway.

Maddie recognized her as the woman who had been looking for Adam outside in the rain.

"We should all get out of here." Maddie directed everybody to the door.

"Alexandra, let's go." Cynthia steered her out of the garage as everyone else followed.

Pierce closed the door behind him.

"What's happened?" Alexandra gasped.

"I'm sorry, it's Adam. He's dead." Cynthia clasped Alexandra's hand.

"Adam. Oh no. What happened?" Instantly, tears began to stream down Alexandra's cheeks.

"What's going on?" Debbie walked down the hallway. She froze at the sight of Alexandra's face.

"Adam. He's dead." Alexandra wiped the tears from her cheeks.

"Dead." Debbie's voice shook. "Who's going to tell Silla?"

"I think she knows." Dirk looked at Silla who stood at the end of the hallway.

"Adam?" A tiny, sweet voice whispered his name just before Silla stepped toward them. "Please, don't let it be true. What happened?"

"We aren't sure, yet. We need to be prepared for all possibilities, just in case," Maddie said.

"Just in case of what?" Debbie sank onto a chair in the hallway. She rubbed the knees of her jeans and rocked back and forth. "In case he finally crossed the wrong person?"

All eyes shifted to Pierce, who still hovered near the garage door.

"What?" Pierce blinked, then wiped water off his face. "It wasn't me. I didn't do anything to him."

"Everyone needs to calm down." Iris held her hands up in the air. Her sopping wet sleeves slid back. "Let's all try to take a deep breath."

"Right now we need to get you out of those wet

clothes." Cynthia looked them over. "I'm sure I can find something for all of you."

"That's very kind of you, Cynthia." Maddie smiled. "It would be good to get into something dry."

"I'm on it." Cynthia started down the hallway.

"I can't believe he's gone. We just met him a short time ago." Katie took a step toward Tammy.

Tammy wrapped her arms around Katie. "At least we found him. With how ferocious the storm is, he could have easily been swept out to sea."

"Speaking of the storm." Dirk looked toward the front door. "I'm going to need to get some more sandbags lined up. If this rain and wind doesn't let up, the bay might end up inside the house."

"I'll help you." Pierce stepped toward him.

"Everyone who can help, should help." Iris glanced around at the others. "We can't have the house flooded, on top of everything else."

"With this many hands, we'll have the house protected in no time." Barbara waved them toward the kitchen. "There are more sandbags in the shed attached to the house out here."

"I'll be right there." Maddie hung back until everyone had followed Barbara. Then she grabbed her phone from her purse. She opened the garage door and stepped back inside as she activated the camera. She crouched down beside Adam's body and pulled one of the towels back to reveal his shoulders and neck. She began snapping pictures of the marks on his neck. His shirt was open enough to see them easily. They encircled his neck as well as the edge of his shoulders. She sent the pictures, along with a text explaining them, to Jake.

As Maddie's heart pounded, she wondered if she simply had an overactive imagination and had seen too many murder mysteries. Maybe it was just an accident. She knew she had to get the information to Jake as soon as possible. But with the storm, would anyone be able to get help to the house? She slid her phone back into her pocket and looked down at her rain-soaked dogs. She stepped back out of the garage and grabbed a towel that had been left out and used it to squeeze the water out of their fur.

"I'm sorry, girls. You probably would have been better off at home. But here we are." Maddie looked up as Cynthia walked in her direction. "Is there somewhere I can leave the dogs, please?"

"Sure." Cynthia pointed down the hall. "First door on the right."

"Thank you." Maddie followed Cynthia's instructions and opened the door to a small bedroom with only a bed and a bedside table inside, on a plush carpet. She left a bowl of water Barbara had fetched, on the floor for them, and they cuddled up on the carpet. "Tired? I'll check on you in a bit." She patted them.

Maddie stepped back into the hallway. Her heart pounded as her mind began to process everything that had happened. It was clear something terrible had happened to Adam, but was it murder? If so, that made everyone in the house a suspect.

As Maddie headed to the kitchen to join the others, she ran through the people she'd met. Clearly there was a problem between Pierce and Adam, and Pierce had been right there when Maddie found Adam's body. That made him a very good suspect. She'd noticed a red mark on his face right near his eye as well that she hadn't noticed when she first met him. If someone murdered Adam, maybe he fought back.

Maddie had just reached the kitchen when her cell phone began to ring. She jumped at the sound. It took her a moment to remember she'd sent a text to Jake. As she answered, she tried to keep her voice calm.

"Hi, Jake. Thanks for getting back to me."

"Getting back to you? Maddie, that's the problem. I can't get to you at all." Jake took a drawn-out breath. "I took a good look at those pictures you sent, and it doesn't look like just an accidental drowning to me. From the marks on his neck and shoulders, I'd guess he was held under the water, which would make it a homicide."

"I guessed that might be the case. What am I supposed to do? How long will it be before you can get out here?"

"I wish I had an answer for you, but right now, the storm is still raging, and it looks like it has stalled over our area. A helicopter won't fly me out there. It's too dangerous in this weather. I'm going to keep trying to find a way to get there, but I think it will be a while before I can get anywhere near Bay Point."

"Hopefully, things will clear up sooner than expected."

"I hope so. Look, Maddie, I know you're going to try to solve this no matter what I say. So, can you please send through everything you find out? You can be my eyes and ears for the start of this investigation. You're always keen to solve a mystery. You always have been. The first few hours in a homicide investigation are very important, and with the water probably washing away any evidence that might be there, you're the best chance I have of getting some idea of what happened to Adam. But please be careful."

"Of course, I'll tell you what I find out, Jake." Maddie was surprised and excited he'd asked for her help. He was right. She would never leave this alone. "But I'm not sure how much I'll find."

"What would help me the most right now is knowing about the people who are in the house. With a storm this bad, my guess is whoever killed Adam is in that house. Can you send me a list of names and anything else you think is important? I'll also speak to the owners and see what they can tell me about who's staying there."

"Yes, absolutely, I'll do that right away." Maddie's heart raced. "I can also talk to the people here and get a feel for what might be going on with them. I already know that another producer, Pierce, and Adam had some kind of falling-out. Also, Adam's girlfriend, Silla, is here. I might be able to find out more about his life from her."

"Just be careful. Try not to be alone with anyone who could have done this. Make sure you're safe."

"I will."

CHAPTER 7

As Maddie tried to focus on what her next step would be, she shivered. She realized she was still wearing her soaking wet clothes. She found a pile of clothing left out by Cynthia to pick through. Once she'd changed into the dry clothes, she joined the others in the dining room where Cynthia had set out coffee and the platter of cupcakes.

The group sipped and chewed in silence, aside from Silla, who whimpered between bites.

"I've been in contact with the chief of police." Maddie drew the attention of everyone in the room. "He's going to get here as soon as he can, but with the roads flooded, it probably won't be until morning."

"We have plenty of rooms for everyone to stay in." Barbara glanced at Cynthia who nodded in agreement. "We know this isn't ideal, but we're all stuck here together, and we want you to be as comfortable as possible."

"Hopefully, the storm will clear up sooner than expected, and the police can start their investigation. I'm sure they'll find this was just a terrible accident." Richard clasped his hands together.

"An accident?" Silla looked up from her cup of coffee. "Adam would never have drowned. He would never risk his life. He's a very good swimmer. This was no accident. Someone did this to him." She glared at Alexandra. "Was it you? Did you do this because he rejected you?"

"Silla, that's not what happened." Alexandra scowled at her and turned away.

"Sure it isn't." Silla stood up. "Any of you could have done this. You were all jealous of Adam and how successful he was." She turned around and left the room.

After a quick but meaningful look at Tammy, Maddie followed after Silla. She knew Tammy would do her best to ensure they had some time alone together, so Maddie could ask Silla some questions.

Silla paused by a large window and looked out through it.

"Silla, I'm so sorry for your loss." Maddie patted her shoulder.

"People will say I have no right to grieve because we were only together for a short time. But he was everything to me, and now he's gone. Not just gone. Someone stole him from me." Silla turned around to face Maddie. Anger inhabited her dark eyes as she continued. "I won't stop until they're caught. Do you hear me? I don't care when the police plan to show up. I'll get to the bottom of this myself."

"And I'll help you in any way I can. You're going through a lot right now. I'm here to help. The best thing you can do at the moment is tell me everything you can about Adam, and especially what his day was like today. Any small detail might be a clue as to how this happened." Maddie searched her eyes. "I assume you were together today?"

"Yes, we were together earlier today. We had a long lunch together in our room."

"I noticed you were running after him when we first arrived. You were trying to speak to him, but he just wanted to be left alone. It seemed as if you'd had an argument," Maddie said.

"No, not at all. He was just upset with Debbie, and he wanted to concentrate on his work. He was very dedicated. He went outside alone." Silla's voice wavered. "Maybe I should have gone after him." She reached up to brush her hair back from her face and revealed a few long scratches on the inside of her wrist. "But just because I think it's a murder, doesn't make it so."

"I agree, it doesn't. But we have to assume it could be. And with the roads flooded, no one can get here to investigate. Like you, I just want to try to find out what happened to him." Maddie looked into her eyes again. "I noticed some tension between Adam and Pierce earlier. Is that something you also noticed?"

"Of course. It was impossible to miss. I mean, they looked like they were going to get into an all-out fistfight when we first arrived."

"And why is that? Did Adam tell you?" Maddie asked.

"He told me his side of the story, but Pierce was more than happy to shout his side. I'm not sure which one is true. All I know is Adam got permission to do this show, and when he showed up, Pierce was already here. Pierce claims he's the one who told Adam about the opportunity, and Adam came in and scooped it out from under Pierce. But Adam insisted he just wanted to include Pierce and he already had a contract with Cynthia and Dirk before he even arrived."

"Is that true? Did you see any paperwork about it?" Maddie did her best to get a clear view of the scratches on her arm.

"I didn't really get involved with the business side of things. He only brought me along because I wanted a few days away. I had planned to just hang out in the room and maybe walk the grounds. But after the confrontation with Pierce, and finding out who Adam got to present the show, I decided to stick close by his side."

"Why? Who did he hire to present the show?"

"Oh, I don't want to talk about that." Silla swept her gaze along the walls near them. "I can tell you this much, though, the stories are true. This place is haunted."

"How do you know that?" Maddie asked.

"I started exploring the house on my own, just out of curiosity. When I went up those back stairs I heard something scraping." Silla pointed to a narrow staircase nearly hidden by a bend in the hallway. "Something heavy, like furniture being moved. Then the light flickered."

"Maybe someone was upstairs moving something? With Pierce and Adam getting everything set up, the electricity might have gone wonky," Maddie said.

"No, you don't understand, Maddie. Those stairs lead to nowhere. Richard says it's an abandoned remodeling project. As for the light flickering, I asked everyone if they had seen it anywhere else in the house, and everyone insisted the lights never flickered. This was long before the storm started." Silla rubbed her hands up and down her arms. "No, there's no explanation for it. Maybe the stories are true, and this place really is haunted."

Maddie fell silent for a moment as she considered her words. "Look, that doesn't really matter either way. The most important thing is finding the murderer. We need to make sure everyone is safe."

"I guess you're right." Silla dropped her hands back to her sides and closed her eyes. "I'm sorry, I've told you everything I know. I need to go lie down for a little while."

"I understand." Maddie glanced at her arm again. "How did you get those scratches?"

"Helping move the equipment inside." Silla waved her hand dismissively as she walked off.

CHAPTER 8

"So, did Silla tell you anything?" Tammy joined Maddie in the hallway, with Amber and Iris a few steps behind her. "Do you think she did it?"

"According to her, everything was good between them." Maddie finished making a note on her phone about the scratches, then waved Katie over as she stepped out of the dining room. "Listen everyone, I know this isn't what we planned on, but we're not getting out of here anytime soon. Jake said he knows I'll want to try to work out who did this to Adam, so he wants me to send him any information I find."

"Oh, that's kind of exciting. We can all help." Katie smiled. "We get to play detective."

"No one is playing anything." Tammy crossed her arms. "This situation is very dangerous."

"Tammy's right. I wonder if we wouldn't be better off taking our chances with the storm." Iris looked between them.

"Absolutely not, Mom!" Amber shot her a stern look. "There's no way we're chancing that weather. It's completely unpredictable."

"All right, everyone, try to relax." Maddie took a deep breath. "We can't go out into the storm. Even if we could make it somewhere safe, we'd be leaving behind people who could be at risk, and I don't know about the rest of you, but I wouldn't be okay with that."

"No, I don't think any of us would be. And I doubt we would make it anywhere safe anyway." Tammy unfolded her arms and surveyed the group of people around her. "But if we're going to try to solve this, we have to be smart about it. If the killer knows we suspect them, they might decide to target us next."

"Exactly." Maddie nodded. "The key is to find out as much information as we can without getting anyone riled up."

"I think Pierce is the first person we should look at. Obviously, they had issues." Amber glanced over her shoulder toward the dining room.

"Okay, I'll talk to him. I can't ask him the questions I want to while he's surrounded by everyone else. I need to get him alone," Maddie said.

"Don't worry about that. I'll get him to you." Amber smiled, confidence brightening her eyes.

"Okay, great." Maddie glanced over at the others gathered around her. "For now, I'd like all of us to try and see what we can find out. Maybe pick a couple of people to try to talk to, but we need to be cautious. We don't know who did this."

"I'll start with Alexandra." Katie raised her hand. "I've seen her work before. I think it'll be easy for us to connect."

"Her work?" Maddie locked eyes with her.

"She's an actress. Apparently, she was hired for the documentary, to be the presenter," Katie said.

"Interesting." Maddie raised an eyebrow. "Silla mentioned something about there being an issue with Adam hiring her, but when I asked her more about it, she just brushed me off. If Alexandra mentions anything about it, let me know."

"I will." Katie nodded.

"I'm sure Debbie and I can strike up a good conversation." Iris smiled. "I like the way she seems to speak everything that's on her mind. She might let something slip that could be helpful."

"Great. Are you okay to talk to Cynthia as well?" Maddie asked.

"Absolutely," Iris said.

"I'll speak to Barbara and Richard." Tammy leaned forward.

"That leaves me with Pierce and Dirk, right? I'll try to speak to them." Amber looked between them. "I'll make sure I make a good impression on them."

"Not too good." Iris pursed her lips. "One of them could be a killer, Amber."

"Don't worry, I'll be careful." Amber kissed her mother's cheek.

"I'm going to try to speak to all of them as well, and I'll keep track of Silla. I did notice she has scratches on her arm. She claims she got them from helping to bring in the equipment, but she doesn't strike me as someone who would have lugged things in from the car." Maddie glanced into the dining room. "All right, Amber, see what you can do to get Pierce into the small room just past the front stairs."

"On it." Amber stepped into the dining room, and instantly, her demeanor took on a lighthearted glow. "Pierce, may I speak with you for a moment? I have so many questions."

"Questions?" Pierce stepped away from the others and settled a puzzled gaze on Amber. "About what?"

"About the show, of course." Amber looped her arm around his and guided him toward the dining room door. "I know there's so much going on right now, and I'm sure you're just heartbroken over Adam's death, but my curiosity is getting the better of me. I grew up in Bayview, you know, and this place has always been said to be haunted by the Becket bride. Is that what you believe?"

Maddie ducked into the small room and waited as she heard them walking down the hall.

"Yes, I do, but there's more to it than that. The Becket bride isn't the only ghost haunting this house. I want to tell the whole story." Pierce paused just outside the door.

"I'd like to hear more about it." Amber gestured through the open doorway.

"All right." Pierce stepped into the room. He stopped when he saw Maddie who stood just past the door.

"Pierce." Maddie took a step toward him. "I was wondering if you had a few minutes."

"What for?" Pierce's gaze swept around the room.

"I just need a few minutes of your time, please. Can you answer a few questions for me?" Maddie noticed that the red mark she had seen on his face earlier had begun turning into a nasty bruise.

"What about?" Pierce turned back toward the door as Amber closed it.

"About what happened to Adam," Maddie said.

"Oh, I see what this is. You want to find out if I hurt Adam." Pierce's voice was filled with venom. "Don't think I'm not aware of how everyone is looking at me. Yes, Adam and I had an argument over what he did to me, but that doesn't mean I killed him!"

CHAPTER 9

*M*addie's heart raced at the anger Pierce displayed. Had she already made a poor decision by being alone in a room with him? He had an injury to his face that occurred around the time Adam was killed. He had plenty of motive to kill him. Yet here she was, in a room alone with an angry potential killer.

"I'm not accusing you of anything. I just want to find out about Adam. I know you and Adam had a falling-out. But I also know you probably knew a few things about him that other people here might not. You two were friends, right?"

"I thought we were." Pierce sighed, then turned away from her. "But I guess I had that wrong."

"Anything you can tell me about Adam, about

what happened today, about the people Adam interacted with, might help us get to the truth about what happened to him." Maddie took a small step closer to Pierce.

He paced slowly back and forth in the small room, from one wall to the other. He shot a sharp glare in her direction. "I don't have to talk to you. You're not a police officer."

"Of course you don't." Maddie took a deep breath as she tried to meet his eyes. "But it would be in your best interest to find out who did this to him. At least that way, you can clear your name. You knew him quite well, and there's that bruise on your cheek. Like you said, it's easy for people to make assumptions about you, since you and Adam were on the outs. At least, that's what I've heard. Is that the truth?"

"I hit myself with my camera." Pierce reached up to touch the bruise. "It was a silly accident. I'd been setting up my own equipment because it's just me. I don't have a whole crew like Adam did. I was trying to mount the camera in a corner of the attic, and it slid out of place and smacked me in the cheek. It doesn't matter what Adam did to me. I didn't have anything to do with his death."

"But what did he do to you?" Maddie stepped

closer, making his space to pace in a bit smaller. "Knowing what was going on between the two of you can only help get closer to the truth. Don't you want the killer caught so none of us are in danger any longer?"

"Of course I want the killer caught, but Adam's murder has nothing to do with me."

"Well, then tell me about it. What harm can it do?"

"I booked this gig. Okay?" Pierce leaned back against the wall. "Adam and I worked together on projects in high school and college. After that, he went one way, and I went another. He found a lot of success, and I'm still struggling. But when I landed this gig, I knew I would get a lot of attention for it. A TV channel agreed to air the show. It's a channel that focuses on horror and supernatural shows. Richard and Barbara have never let anyone film here, ever. But now that the grandkids took over, I guess they're more relaxed about these things."

"So, you would have been the first to film here?"

"Yes. I guess, I just wanted to brag about it a little. I wanted him to see I was doing something great, and my show would be aired. He didn't even really care about paranormal stuff, but I still wanted to brag. I invited him to lunch, and we talked about the project. He was impressed, like I'd hoped he would be."

"But things went awry?"

"I came here to do the show and was getting all set up when Adam showed up." Pierce's jaw tensed. "He produced this paperwork saying he had gotten the rights from the family of the man who's haunting this house. Vincent Maller. He died here about forty years ago, and his ghost haunts the house. Adam had exclusive rights. So, what that meant was I could film the house and interview the owners, but I couldn't mention a single thing about Vincent. Without that, there isn't even much of a story. The TV channel never would have aired it. He'd heard my idea and gone around to ensure he would be the only one who could produce this."

"That must have made you so angry."

"Yes, of course it made me angry. But he tried to play the hero, as usual. He told me we could make the show together. I wouldn't get full credit, but he would include my name. I knew it would at least still give me some perks and potential future jobs, so I agreed to it." Pierce scowled as he looked back at her. "He threw me a bone when he didn't have to. So, why would I kill him?"

"Killing him would open the opportunity to get

the rights to Vincent's story, wouldn't it? I would think that would be very beneficial for you."

"No, you're wrong. That would have taken time, and money for lawyers, neither of which I have. The best thing would have been for me to be able to get the documentary aired, including details of Vincent. When that couldn't happen, the next best thing would have been for Adam to release it, so at least I would get some publicity. Now I can't do anything, at least not until I jump through a ton of legal hoops. This is all bad for me. I can only do the show without mentioning Vincent at all. That's what I have to work with. And like I said, the TV channel will never air it." Pierce clenched his jaw. "So, your sleuthing skills are a little off. I had no reason to kill him."

"No reason other than revenge or rage." Maddie took a step toward him. "Sometimes people don't think things through. Sometimes they're just so angry, they act, even if it will hurt them in the long run."

"No." Pierce raised his voice. "I would never do something like that. No matter what he did to me. I'm innocent. Look, I need to go. I want to start filming, if they'll let me. Maybe I can at least get some footage I can put on my social media." He walked out of the room.

As Maddie followed him out into the hallway, she found him frozen just outside the door. His flushed cheeks had drained of all color as he stared hard at the other end of the hallway.

"Did you see that?" Pierce pointed.

"See what?" Maddie peered down the hallway in the same direction.

"I could have sworn..." Pierce swallowed hard, then shook his head. "Never mind. It doesn't matter." He started to walk away.

"Hold on," Maddie called out.

Pierce glanced back to look at her, his eyes huge.

"What did you see, Pierce?"

"I wanted to do this documentary so badly because I believe in the ghost stories. And I think I just saw one walk by." Pierce turned back around and strode off.

As Maddie watched him, she thought about their conversation. He claimed his innocence, but she found it hard to believe he didn't hold a grudge. He remained high on her suspect list.

CHAPTER 10

*D*etermined to get to the truth, Maddie decided to speak with Alexandra. She'd been out in the rain looking for Adam shortly before his body washed up. Maybe she'd found him and had a reason to kill him.

Maddie walked down the hallway and found Cynthia rushing toward her.

"Cynthia, how are you doing with everything? Do you need any help?"

"Oh, no, thank you. We've almost got all the rooms set up." Cynthia rubbed her forehead. "There's just so much to do with the storm and add to that what happened to Adam."

"It must be very stressful."

"It is." Cynthia gave a short laugh. "But nothing we can't handle. I think I'm going to head to the kitchen and have another of your cupcakes. Comfort food."

"Absolutely." Maddie realized that she wouldn't mind another cupcake herself. "I'm glad you're enjoying them. Let me know if I can help you with anything."

"Thank you."

"I'm looking for Alexandra. Have you seen her?" Maddie asked.

"Yes. She was heading that way." Cynthia pointed toward the back of the house.

"Thank you." Maddie started in that direction. She found Alexandra in the screened-in back porch, staring out at the rain that still fell. "Alexandra?"

"Hmm?" Alexandra turned toward her with a mug clutched between her palms. "Oh, Maddie, right?"

"Right." Maddie stepped farther onto the porch. "How are you doing?"

"How should I be doing?" Alexandra looked back out at the rain. "We're all in the same boat, stuck here, and Adam is dead."

"You knew Adam well? He was your boss. Or

were you two friends as well?" Maddie walked up to the screen and also peered outside. The patter of the raindrops sounded a little more spaced out. She felt a burst of hope that the storm might be passing.

"Not friends, no. Well, maybe I thought we were." Alexandra ran her hand across her forehead. "I can't make sense of any of it. How can he be dead?"

"It's shocking." Maddie studied the woman's expression. "Had you known him for a long time?"

"Sort of. We knew each other a while ago, then fell out of touch. When he reached out to me to hire me for this job, he said it was because he knew I would be perfect for the part." Alexandra took a sip from the mug she held, then licked her lips. "I guess because I had told him all about my grandmother's habit of giving everyone tea leaf readings."

"So, you're familiar with the spiritual side of things?" Maddie smiled.

"A bit. My grandmother was into it, but my mother insisted that she keep me out of it. I guess she had some experiences as a child that frightened her. Let's just say my grandmother didn't follow the rules, so I had some experiences of my own."

"Why were you looking for Adam earlier?"

"Because I wanted to apologize. Actually, grovel. I did something impulsive as usual, and I was hoping to undo it."

"In the pouring rain? What did you do that was that bad?" Maddie asked.

"I quit." Alexandra pursed her lips and gripped the mug tightly.

"Why? Did he do something to upset you?"

"Yes. I thought when he hired me for this job that he really respected me and my work. I thought he hired me because of my talent. But that's not why."

"Tell me what happened." Maddie softened her voice.

"To you, it may seem like nothing. But to me, it was huge. I was getting ready to start filming, and he walked into my room." Alexandra glanced up at Maddie as crimson tinged her cheeks. "I had just been psyching myself up, telling myself how much I deserved this role and how I'd earned it with all of my hard work. I had been building up my confidence, so it would show when the camera started rolling. But when he came into my room, all of that changed."

"How did it change?" Maddie watched the way

Alexandra shifted her gaze around the room. She looked at everything but Maddie.

"He started out being nice, complimenting me on how I looked and saying how glad he was I would be part of the show." Alexandra sighed. "The whole time, I really thought he'd invited me to be part of this project because he believed in my talent."

"Didn't he?" Maddie narrowed her eyes. "What happened?"

"We dated, a few years back. He was single then. It was just a quick relationship, no more than a week or two. We both moved on without an issue. When he invited me here, I knew he had a girlfriend, so I didn't think there would be anything between us. But apparently he had another idea. When he came into my room, he made it very clear that he invited me here for another reason. He said he wanted to go out with me. He even tried to kiss me." Alexandra cringed. "When I stopped him and pointed out he had a girlfriend, and it wouldn't be right, he said it didn't matter, it would be our secret. I was so angry. I felt so disappointed that he hadn't invited me here because of my talent. He just thought he could take advantage of me. How was I supposed to be okay with that?"

"I can understand why you would be so angry. So, you turned him down? Is that why you quit?"

"Yes, I told him I would never go out with him while he was dating Silla. He said something about my job depending on it, so I told him he could take the job and shove it." Alexandra snapped her words. "He apologized when he saw I was serious. He told me he was just joking, and we could forget any of it happened. But I refused to accept his apology and told him I would be leaving. He stormed off." She stared up at the ceiling. "When I had time to think, I realized I was being impulsive. The person I was hurting the most was me. Being part of the show with his name on it would help my career. And I need the money. So, I decided that as long as he wouldn't ask anything unprofessional of me, I would do the job. But at that point, I had to hope he would still be willing to give it back to me. So, I went out to find him."

"You must have still been angry, though. After what he did, you had every right to be. Maybe when you found him, when you saw him again, it all just came pouring out. You already said you act on impulse sometimes."

"I didn't kill him. I would never hurt anyone. Besides, I never found him." Alexandra brushed past her, toward the door that led inside the house. "If you want to suspect someone, talk to Dirk and Cynthia. They've been arguing ever since I arrived. I didn't really hear exactly what they said, but I did hear them say something to do with Adam and the documentary. They might act all sweet and nice, but I've heard them saying some vicious things."

CHAPTER 11

addie started toward the kitchen. Cynthia had mentioned she was going to get another cupcake. Maybe she would still be there. When Maddie stepped into the kitchen, she caught sight of Dirk and Cynthia arguing in front of the large kitchen window.

"Look, it must have been something to do with Vincent." Dirk's stern tone conflicted with the friendly man she'd first met.

They both fell silent as Maddie stepped farther into the kitchen.

"Is everything okay here?" Maddie looked between them. "Listen, you can talk to me. Whatever you're thinking, whatever you might know, you can tell me. If we put our heads together, we might be able to solve this murder." She paused a few steps away from them. "What about Vincent? He died here almost forty years ago, didn't he?"

"Yes." Richard's voice drifted in from the doorway. He walked inside the kitchen, followed by Barbara.

"What happened to Vincent?" Maddie looked at Richard and Barbara. "You two owned the house when it happened, right? Wasn't he a friend of yours?"

"Yes, we owned it. Actually, the three of us owned it. We were all good friends at the time. We planned for it to be a boardinghouse. But when we realized the Becket bride haunted it, we decided to open it as a haunted B&B. And now Vincent haunts the house as well." Richard lowered his voice and glanced around the room as if someone might be listening. "The bride. She's the one who killed him."

"You think the Becket bride killed Vincent? A ghost?" Maddie recalled the night she'd run from Becket House. "What is the whole story about her?"

"The legend goes that a groom, Bob Becket, built this house for his bride, but he'd never met her before. It was an arranged marriage, and she was coming from overseas to marry him. When she arrived, she hated everything about the climate, the people, the house, and even her husband. He still forced her to marry him, and they had a very rocky relationship," Cynthia explained.

"She would spend her days in the attic. She would be seen in the attic window, just staring out," Barbara said.

"Until one day, she was found dead. The details of her death are sketchy. But it's believed her husband murdered her." Richard narrowed his eyes. "It's hard to decipher what really happened because it was so long ago, and we can't find any records."

"And now she haunts this house." Barbara gestured around her.

"I don't understand what that has to do with Vincent," Maddie said.

"Vincent fell off the roof." Cynthia lowered her voice to a whisper. "But a few people said they saw the ghost of the bride on the roof with him. It's believed she must have chased him out there, but of course, nothing could be proven."

"So, the story is that the ghost of the bride killed Vincent?" Maddie could see the seriousness in all of their expressions.

"Yes. It's the only thing that makes sense. I could never understand why Vincent was on the roof. He had no reason to be there. Not unless someone chased him out there." Barbara snapped her fingers. "Either the Becket bride somehow pushed him, or she scared him so badly that he slipped. Either way, she's responsible for his death."

Maddie didn't want to agree with them, but she knew what she herself had seen in that window. Maybe it wasn't just her imagination. But it couldn't have been a ghost. She didn't believe in ghosts.

"And now you think Vincent haunts this house, too?"

"Yes, his room was kept exactly as it was when he died." Barbara glanced at Cynthia. "But when I'd go in there to dust, I'd find his things moved around. Sometimes his covers are pulled back as if he slept in his bed."

"It's been the same for me since we took over the place. Often, we'll hear footsteps coming from his room above us at night. It's hard to deny it when it's almost a daily occurrence." Cynthia shrugged.

"Someone said they heard you arguing about doing the documentary." Maddie looked at Cynthia and Dirk. They glanced at each other, then looked back at Maddie.

"Oh, I wouldn't say we were arguing. It was more of a discussion." Cynthia cleared her throat. "Richard and Barbara didn't want us to do the show, but we thought the exposure would be good for the business. We were discussing whether it was the right decision, that's all. But if only we hadn't agreed to it, Adam would still be alive."

"And like I told you, Cynthia, you shouldn't blame yourself." Dirk patted her hand.

"Okay, enough of this. We can't stand around chatting while the storm is raging." Barbara turned toward the door. "We're going to check on the sandbags. The latest weather update is that the rain may lighten up a bit for an hour or so, but we may still be looking at some heavier bands coming through after that."

"Great." Maddie cringed at the thought of even more rain flooding the area.

CHAPTER 12

As Maddie stepped out of the kitchen, her cell phone rang. Jake's name danced across the screen.

"Hello?"

"Maddie, how's it going?"

Maddie smiled at the sound of his voice. "Nowhere, really. I've spoken with almost everyone, and I'm no closer to finding the murderer than I was when I started."

"You've spoken to most of the people in the house?"

"Yes." Maddie walked down the hallway where she wouldn't be overheard.

"That's fantastic. I thought maybe you would

have spoken to a few, but almost everyone, that's great. It'll give us a good place to start."

Maddie could tell from the tone of his voice that he was smiling.

"Just tell me what you think are the most important things you learned," Jake said.

Maddie shared with him the notes she'd made.

"Interesting. It sounds like quite a few people had a pretty good motive, but both Pierce and Alexandra were outside around the time he was killed. That's very important information," Jake said.

"Do you know much about Vincent Maller and his death?"

"No, not much. There was a report from a few people saying they saw someone with Vincent on the roof just before he died, but they couldn't find the person, and nothing was ever proven. I think the fact the witnesses said it was a ghost made the reports not be taken that seriously. That's why I didn't want you to go out there in the first place. I've heard the reports about Vincent's death not being accidental, and the other stories about that place are crazy. I'm going to look deeper into the records about Vincent's death to see if there's anything else I can find there."

"And you definitely think Adam was murdered?" Maddie could hear Jake shuffling some papers.

"Yes, it looks like someone held him under the water. He might have fought back. The person who did this might have some bruising or scratches on their hands or arms."

"I noticed that Silla has scratches on her arms. Do you think she would be strong enough to do this?"

"From what you've told me about her, I don't think it's likely she could hold him down. But maybe if he had passed out? We don't know what his state was before he went into the water."

"I also noticed that Pierce had a bruise on his cheek," Maddie said.

"It's possible Adam swung an arm hard enough to strike Pierce in the face."

"I'll let you know if I find out anything else."

"Okay, but remember to be careful."

"I will be." Maddie ended the call.

As she walked out into the hall, Tammy walked toward her. Maddie had a feeling she was keeping an eye on her, to make sure she wasn't alone and putting herself in danger.

"What are you up to?" Tammy asked.

"I just got off the phone with Jake. You know, I was just thinking, we took Adam's raincoat off to make it easier to get him out of the water. I might have a look through his pockets. Maybe there's something there," Maddie suggested.

"It's worth a try. I'll come with you."

"Thanks." Maddie started down the hallway toward the front door. She had seen Cynthia hang Adam's raincoat up in a small room off the entrance. Maddie pulled out a pair of latex gloves from her pocket and put them on.

"You have gloves?" Tammy followed Maddie into the room.

"Yes, in case I need to put pastries on display." Maddie laughed. "Never know when they might come in handy."

Maddie walked over to the raincoat hanging on a hook on the wall and unzipped the pockets. She put her hand in one. After she found nothing, she checked the other. She immediately touched something and pulled it free.

"It's a folded piece of paper. It's not too wet because it was in the pocket of his raincoat, but it's still damp." She started to unfold the paper.

"Don't open it yet." Tammy touched Maddie's

hand. "Let it dry out completely first. I saw that on a true crime show once. Just keep it with you. It could be important, or it could be nothing. Anything else?"

"A lighter." Maddie held up the item.

"Was Adam a smoker?"

"No, I don't think so. But Debbie is. Adam even said to her it was a bad habit."

"That's right." Tammy nodded.

"And this lighter is covered in flowers and bright colors. It looks more like something a woman would choose."

"Maybe he took it from Debbie? Or she gave it to him?" Tammy suggested.

"Maybe. I'll hang on to it." Maddie wrapped the lighter in a tissue and put it in her pocket. "It's probably not related to the murder, but who knows."

As Maddie walked with Tammy toward the door, she recalled the scratches on Silla's arm. Her size made it less likely she could be the killer, but Maddie had been through enough in life to know never to make assumptions. She could have tricked him. Or maybe she knocked him out first. But why would someone who claimed to be his girlfriend want to kill him? She recalled the conversation she'd had with Alexandra. Had Silla found out that Adam made a move on Alexandra? Had Silla lost it and killed Adam because of it?

CHAPTER 13

"*I* just want to check on Bella and Polly."
Maddie and Tammy stepped out of the
room off the entrance.

"What were you doing in there?" Amber called
out from behind them.

"We looked in Adam's coat pockets." Maddie
explained what they had found.

"Interesting. I wonder what's on the paper."
Amber narrowed her eyes.

"Hopefully, we can find out soon." Tammy
started toward the room the dogs were in.

"From the forecast, the rain should lighten up
for a bit, and then the weather is only going to get
worse. I want to go outside and have a look around
the area Adam washed up in. I might be able to find

something that proves who was there with him or find a clue about who killed him." Maddie opened the door. The dogs ran over to greet them with wagging tails as they bent down to pat them.

"You really want to go outside?" Amber winced. "The wind is still howling."

"She's right, but the rain isn't too bad." Katie stepped through the still open door with Iris right behind her. "I just stuck my head outside to see, and it's almost down to a drizzle."

"Still, it can't be safe with all the flooding. I don't think it's a good idea." Tammy rubbed the dogs' bellies as they rolled over.

"Listen, if there's anything to find out there, it might disappear with the next band of rain that comes through." Maddie walked to the window and looked outside at the drops of rain that struck the glass. "I think we need to have a look before every bit of evidence is destroyed."

"I also don't think that's such a good idea." Iris gazed out through the window as well. "We don't know what this storm might decide to do. It's already proven itself to be very unpredictable. It's dark, and the next band might come sooner than expected. What if you get lost out there in the dark?"

"I'll be okay." Maddie shrugged.

"You can't go alone. I'll go with you, Aunt Maddie." Katie stepped forward the same second that her mother spoke up.

"Absolutely not! You will stay right here, Katie. I'll go with Maddie." Tammy wrapped her arm around her sister's. "I'll keep her safe."

"But, Mom, you can't go out there." Katie glared at her. "What if you get hurt? If I can't go, then you can't go."

"None of us should be going." Iris crossed her arms. "I don't have a good feeling about it."

"I'm sorry, Iris." Maddie turned toward her. "I know your instincts are usually great, but I don't want to take the chance that the killer will get away with this or kill someone else because I didn't bother to look for evidence. If it's too bad, I'll forget about it and come back inside."

"I'll go with you, Maddie," Amber squeaked out her words as she squirmed under her mother's heavy gaze.

"Amber. You can't." Iris reached for her daughter.

"Mom, I'm a grown woman." Amber brushed her mother's hand away from her arm. "I'm capable of making my own choices and taking my own risks. This is one I'm willing to take."

"Well, if you're going, I'm going." Iris crossed her arms.

"If they're going, I'm going." Katie crossed her arms as well.

"I can't believe this!" Tammy threw her hands up into the air. "Fine, we'll all go. I might just have to tie a rope around us to keep us all from floating away, though," she grumbled.

After making sure the dogs had enough water and were settled, they headed back out of the room.

"Don't worry, the moment I see that storm picking up again, I'm hauling all of you back inside." Iris stepped through the door that Tammy held open for her.

Amber and Maddie exchanged a wry smile before joining them, with Katie just behind. Once outside, they each turned on the flashlight on their phones.

"Even with this light, I can't see much. What do you really think we'll find, Maddie?" Tammy sloshed through the water that swirled around her feet.

"No idea, but it's worth having a look. Maybe there's a clue. Maybe when Adam came out here to make some audio recordings, he discovered something. Or maybe he wasn't out here just to do some recordings. Maybe he was looking for something." Maddie scanned the light from her phone across some grass sticking out of the water as they continued uphill.

"What do you think he could have been out here looking for?" Iris studied the grass as well.

"Probably nothing." Maddie sighed as she neared another patch of almost uncovered grass. "Maybe I'm just desperate for answers."

"Well, this is interesting." Katie pointed her light at a pile of trash bags farther up the hill. "Why wouldn't this be in the garbage instead of just thrown into a pile like this?"

"Good question." Maddie lifted up the edge of the trash bag and aimed the flashlight inside. "There're all kinds of light bulbs and electrical stuff. It's an odd place for these to be."

"Yes, it is." Amber crouched down to take a closer look. "Do you think they all came from the house?"

"They must have. It's the only building for miles. I don't think anyone would have dumped it here. The road is all the way on the other side." Iris shielded her eyes as the rain began to come down harder. "I think we'd better leave it here for now. I don't think we can get it all back to the house with the storm as bad as it is."

"I'll grab some pictures." Tammy began snapping photographs of the equipment in the bags.

"Do you think this might have been what Adam was looking for? Or maybe he just stumbled across it?" Katie tried to meet Maddie's eyes through the rain.

"I have no idea." Maddie gasped as she felt a rush of water swirl up to her ankles. "I think we need to get out of this area. The water is getting deeper."

"Absolutely." Tammy grabbed Katie's arm and tugged her away from the water.

"Let's go!" Amber grabbed on to her mother's hand, and they all backed away from the water.

As they turned toward the B&B, Katie shrieked.

"Who is that?" She pointed through the sheets of rain in the direction of the attic window. "Please tell me I'm not the only one seeing that."

Maddie froze at the sight of the stark white face in the window. She recognized the flowing blonde hair. The same image she had seen all those years ago. She caught a glimpse of what she thought was white lace covering the woman's shoulders. Was it really the ghost of the Becket bride? How could it be?

"It must be the rain playing tricks on us." Tammy bit into her bottom lip. "It's shadows and reflections. It's nothing."

"It's moving." Amber watched as the face moved away from the window.

"Tammy's right. We all just need to get inside. I'm sure there's an explanation for whatever we just saw." Iris continued toward the house.

They battled against the onslaught of heavy raindrops to make it to the front door.

CHAPTER 14

irk waited for them in the open doorway of the house, his eyes wide and his voice loud.

"What were you thinking going out there?" He waved them inside. "It's dangerous!"

"Have you lost your minds?" Barbara appeared moments later with a stack of fresh towels. "You had us all in a panic."

"Sorry about that." Maddie heaved a sigh of relief as the wind and rain were silenced by the door that closed behind her. "We were hoping we might be able to find some evidence out there before the storm washed it all away."

"You must be freezing." Barbara draped a towel

around Maddie's shoulders. "Come on, I'll get you all some dry clothes to put on."

After they'd all changed, for the second time in one day, Maddie walked down the hall. She noticed Cynthia walking toward her.

"Cynthia, I think we should get everyone together in the dining room."

"Why?"

"I think we need to have a real conversation about what happened to Adam. Everyone should be kept apprised of what is happening," Maddie said.

"All right, I'll gather everyone together." Cynthia turned around.

Within moments, the others had filed into the dining room, filling in the large, dark wooden chairs and picking at the remains of the cupcakes Maddie had delivered.

Tammy hovered nearby but didn't sit. Her gaze lingered on Maddie.

Maddie could feel it as she took a deep breath.

"All right, everyone, I think it's time we all faced the truth about what is happening here. It has become very clear Adam's death was no accident. Someone killed him." She watched the expressions of the people gathered around her. Maybe they would reveal something.

Silla lowered her head into her hands and began to cry. Alexandra pursed her lips as she stared at the table. Pierce sighed heavily and looked up at the ceiling.

Debbie winced but remained quiet as she pulled a pack of cigarettes from her pocket.

Richard grabbed his wife's hand as they sat on a couch.

Dirk and Cynthia hovered in the doorway.

"So, you're saying someone here killed him?" Barbara looked around the room. "Someone in this room?"

"That's one possibility." Maddie cleared her throat.

"What do you mean it's one possibility? Obviously no one could survive outside in this storm. So, the killer has to be here!" Barbara snapped.

"I agree, the killer has to be in the house." Maddie swept her gaze around the room again. "But not necessarily in this room."

"I knew it," Barbara moaned. "It's Vincent, isn't it?"

"Vincent, the dead guy?" Alexandra's eyes widened.

"Are you serious?" Tammy crossed her arms as

she looked around the large dining room. "The best we can come up with is a ghost? How does a ghost drown someone anyway?"

"I know it sounds far-fetched, especially to people who haven't been living in a haunted house for years." Barbara held up her hands and sighed. "But none of us can get out of here. We're stuck here. And that means we're all in danger."

"Yes, you're right, we're all in danger." Iris pursed her lips. "Because there's a murderer in this house with us, a flesh-and-blood one. The more time we waste on this discussion about a ghost, the better chance there is the murderer will kill again. So, please, drop this ridiculous idea!"

"It's not ridiculous." Cynthia glared at Iris so fiercely that Amber stepped between them.

"Everyone take a breath." Amber held up her hands in a surrendering gesture. "This isn't getting us anywhere. We're all stuck here. That's all we know for sure. It's possible there's a killer in this house with us. You can also believe the killer is a ghost. My point is it doesn't matter. It doesn't matter what we believe. What matters is that we have to stay safe."

"How can we stay safe? We can't go anywhere."

Debbie threw her hands up as her voice rose. "This whole place is flooded."

"Everybody, calm down. We just need to ride out the storm," Maddie called out. "We're going to be fine. I'm going to try and get hold of the chief and see if he has any new information on when the police can get here or when we can get out of here. You all should stay here together."

"You can't force us to stay here." Debbie jumped to her feet. "We'll be like sitting ducks."

"Whoever the killer is probably only wanted Adam dead." Iris waved her hand through the air. "They wouldn't take the chance of killing more people. There's safety in numbers."

"You know Adam didn't turn up dead until after you all showed up. How do we know none of you is the killer?" Debbie pointed at Maddie and her friends.

"She has a point." Pierce raised his eyebrows. "How do we know none of you had a reason to kill Adam?"

"Feel free to investigate us all you want. Iris will give you all of our names. While you're doing that, I'm going to contact the chief." Maddie turned around and started down the hallway.

"Maddie. Wait up." Amber followed after her, with Katie and Tammy close behind.

"What are you really up to?" Tammy asked.

"You saw what I saw in that attic." Maddie looked at them.

They all nodded.

"I want to search this house. I want to try to find out if anyone is hiding in it. I want to find out exactly what happened here," Maddie said.

"We should start our search in the attic." Amber looked toward the stairs.

"You and Maddie start in the attic. Katie and I will start on the first floor, and we'll meet in the middle." Tammy caught Maddie by the arm. "Be careful!"

"You both be careful, too." Maddie gave them each a quick hug, then walked off with Amber toward the sweeping staircase in the middle of the entranceway. She paused at the bottom of the stairs and looked over at Amber. "The face we all just saw in the attic window is the same face I saw when we were kids. I saw it in the window then, too. I don't know how to explain it, Amber, but whatever we saw is definitely spooky."

"So, you think it's a ghost?" Amber's voice took on a high-pitched tone.

"I don't know what to think. I don't believe in ghosts. What I do know is that if it's a person, they might have left a clue behind. It's possible there's another person in this house, and we don't know about it. As large as this place is, someone could easily hide in here. I want to know who was looking out that window," Maddie said.

"Then let's go." Amber hooked her arm around Maddie's and mounted the steps.

CHAPTER 15

As Maddie and Amber climbed the stairs to the attic, Maddie's mind flashed back to that night when she was a teenager. It couldn't have been the same face. It was impossible. Wasn't it?

"Maddie, are you going to go in?" Amber gave her a light nudge on the back of her shoulder. "You're not scared, are you?"

"No, of course not." Maddie cleared her throat. "Why would I be? There's only a murderer roaming the house."

"That's not what I meant." Amber lowered her voice. "I mean, you're not scared about what you saw that night, are you? What we all saw today?"

"I'm not scared. Like I said, I don't understand it."

"Tell me, did you really see that same face we saw in the window today? Are you sure?" Amber asked.

"Yes, I think so." Maddie took a step forward into the attic.

"Anyone in there?" Pierce shouted from just behind them. "I'm warning you now, I'm armed and not afraid to use it!"

Maddie jumped, then spun around to face him. "Is that true? Are you armed?"

Pierce put his finger to his lips, then shook his head.

"What are you doing here?" Amber hissed. "You're supposed to be with the others."

"Look, I thought you might search the attic after what you saw, and I can't let four women go off on their own in search of a murderer. Okay? What kind of man would I be if I did that?" Pierce put his hands on his hips.

"Shh!" Maddie turned back to the attic. She pointed her flashlight into the darkness. The column of light captured dust particles and hanging cobwebs. The darkness vanished a second later as the attic flooded with light.

"I found the switch." Amber beamed with pride.

"Good job." Maddie's gaze swept over the

expanse of the attic. The large space appeared to be filled to the brim with boxes and old furniture. She looked at Amber. "Let's see what we can find. There are lots of places someone could hide up here."

"We're not afraid of you," Pierce called from the doorway. "You'd better come out now because we're going to find you either way!"

For a moment, all three of them fell silent before Maddie took a step forward. She moved toward a tall pile of boxes she guessed someone could hide behind. As she stepped around them, a sudden movement caused her to jerk to the side. She gasped as a mouse bolted over her foot. She bumped into the pile of boxes while trying to catch her balance, and the stack tumbled to the ground.

The contents of the boxes slid across the wooden floor. A large, glossy photograph skidded to a stop at Amber's feet.

"Oh my gosh!" She stared down at the photograph of a man.

"Vincent!" Pierce crouched down to look at the photograph as Maddie hurried over to them. "It's him for sure. I've been studying the history of the place." He looked up at the rafters of the attic. "Is it you up here, Vincent? Are you trying to tell us something?"

"It's not him. I just knocked some boxes over. We need to be looking for any sign someone might be hiding out." Maddie froze at the sight of something else on the floor, a piece of paper with Vincent's name printed on it. "What's this?" As she began to read it over, she picked it up. "It looks like some kind of business agreement between Barbara, Richard, and Vincent." She narrowed her eyes. "It shows they all had an equal share in the house."

"Is everything okay in here?" Richard stepped through the attic door, his brow knitted with concern. "We all heard the crash downstairs."

"We're okay. Sorry, I just bumped into some boxes." Maddie pointed at the boxes.

"What are you doing up here?" Richard asked.

"We wanted to see if anyone was hiding out. Did you keep Vincent's paperwork?" Maddie looked at the papers.

"We kept everything." Richard pursed his lips. "Losing Vincent was like losing a member of our family. We had a hard time letting anything go. But you three are wasting your time up here. There's nothing to find."

"Nothing?" Maddie raised her eyebrows. "I'm certain someone was in this attic. I'm not the only one who saw a person looking out the window."

"A person?" Richard looked over at one of the large windows, then looked back at Maddie. "Oh, you must have seen the ghost of Celeste." He gestured to a large painting propped against one of the walls. It was of a young woman with long, blonde hair and bright blue eyes. "This is Celeste, or at least an artist's depiction of what she looked like. She's the bride we told you about. You must have seen her ghost. I know you don't all believe it, but that's the truth."

"Maybe what we saw outside was a reflection of this painting?" Amber quirked an eyebrow.

"That seems impossible." Maddie shook her head.

"More impossible than a ghost?" Amber crossed her arms.

"Maybe not. But I still think an actual person is the best explanation," Maddie said.

"I know some people find it hard to believe in ghosts, but trust me, Celeste is haunting this house." Richard looked at the painting. "I keep telling Barbara if we get rid of everything to do with Celeste, her ghost might somehow finally rest, but she says this house was built for Celeste, and some piece of her should stay here."

"Maybe it was a reflection of the painting. I still

think it's possible it was an actual person, though." Maddie locked eyes with Amber. "Why don't you all go back downstairs, and I'll clean up the mess I made. I'll be right down."

"All right." Amber nodded, as if she understood Maddie's true intentions.

Once they had left, Maddie began digging through the box in search of more information about the house. Maybe, somehow, there was some kind of clue in the boxes of who they'd seen in the attic.

CHAPTER 16

$\mathcal{M}$addie snapped pictures of what she'd found about Vincent and the relationship between him, Richard, and Barbara. The documents indicated Vincent was trying to make sure his ownership of Becket House would be retained even if his friendship with Richard and Barbara was not. It looked as if he was making responsible business-related choices to protect himself in the long run.

Maddie guessed that someone who went into business with a married couple might want to take some extra steps to protect their part in it. One particular piece of paper held her attention. It was handwritten questions about the story of the Becket bride. She couldn't be sure whose handwriting it was, but the questions were about the validity of the information. What country did she come from? Where were the marriage records? Who could verify her existence?

Was it Vincent's handwriting? Did he question the story? Or did he want to provide all the information to the people who stayed at the B&B?

"Everyone! Downstairs! Now!" Dirk's voice boomed through the house.

Maddie jumped to her feet and rushed down the steps to the first floor. "What's wrong? What's happening?"

Cynthia met her at the kitchen door.

"The water is coming inside through the front door more now. We need to act fast to protect the house and keep all of us safe. There are more sandbags in the shed attached to the house." She turned toward a small hallway in the kitchen that led to the back door. "We just have to stick close to the house. We shouldn't get too wet."

Everyone put on raincoats.

"You wait here." Maddie moved ahead of Cynthia to the door. Dirk had pushed it open. "We'll make an assembly line and pass the sandbags along. There will be less chance of someone slipping that way."

"Good idea." Silla took a position right beside the door. "I'll take them from Dirk and pass them to Cynthia, who can pass them to you."

"I can help." Pierce shouldered his way past the three women and stepped outside. "Let's go. The wind is fierce."

Maddie followed him and held her hands out to grab the first sandbag from Cynthia. When she turned to carry it to Pierce, who was close to the front door, she found Tammy right beside her.

Tammy took the bag and passed it to Amber, who passed it right to Katie, who passed it to Pierce. Within a few minutes, all the sandbags had been moved and lined up outside the front door, and they all hurried back inside.

"Hopefully, that will be enough to keep the water at bay for a little while." Dirk brushed off his palms, then glanced at the others gathered around him. "I don't think the police are going to be able to get out here at all tonight. There are plenty of rooms available if you all want to pick somewhere to sleep."

"Sleep?" Alexandra raised her eyebrows. "How can we possibly do that with a murderer roaming around?"

"I know it won't be easy, but our bodies need

rest whether we like it or not. There's plenty of food in the kitchen, so help yourselves. I'm exhausted." Dirk yawned. "I'm going to try to get an hour or two, then I'll get up and check on the flooding. As long as you're all here, you're our guests, and I can assure you Cynthia and I will do our best to keep you safe and as comfortable as possible."

"I can't believe I'm stuck here." Alexandra gestured around her. "I never should have trusted Adam. I never should have come here."

"That makes two of us. But since I'm stuck here, do you mind if I make some more recordings?" Pierce shifted his attention to Cynthia. "I might be able to salvage some kind of show out of this, if I have your permission."

"Sure, record whatever you'd like." Cynthia waved her hand dismissively as she followed Dirk to the stairs. "Everyone should sleep upstairs, just in case the flooding really gets out of control."

"We're going to get some sleep as well." Richard started toward the stairs with Barbara's hand clasped in his.

Maddie glanced over at the thin streams of water seeping in under the front door. Her heart lurched at the thought of a deluge of water rushing inside.

"Can we all stay together?" Amber rubbed her arms as she looked around at their small group. "This place unnerves me."

"Sure, let's go get some food." Tammy linked her arm through Amber's.

"I'll get the pups some food as well." Katie walked with Tammy and Amber toward the kitchen.

"So, it's just you and me, kid." Iris' eyes shone as she looked straight at Maddie. "How are you holding up? I know you didn't really want to come here after what you saw in that attic all those years ago."

"I'm fine. Now, at least I have an explanation for what it was. She was probably just a reflection of the painting."

"Is that what you really think?" Iris searched her eyes.

"I still think it might have been a person. But it was probably just a reflection of the painting. It wasn't a ghost. I know that much."

"Okay, well at least you can put that all behind you now." Iris smiled.

"Exactly." Maddie recalled the day all those years ago. The woman she had seen in the attic had waved at her. Obviously, she'd just embellished the memory over the years. Paintings can't wave.

Maybe it was the shadows. Like today, it was cloudy, casting eerie shadows over the house. "Anyway, right now, I have to focus on finding a killer, not an imaginary ghost. I need to get the girls. I can't leave them down here in case the water breaks through."

"Yes, of course."

"Thanks for listening, Iris. It means a lot to have you all here with me." Maddie gave her a quick hug and smiled as she recalled the numerous times she'd found herself in Iris' warm arms. After Maddie's father had died, Iris was always there to comfort her and her sister, especially when her mother was too engrossed in her grief. Any time they faced a crisis, Iris would pick up the pieces, even when she worried about what wild thing Maddie might rope Amber into.

As Maddie pulled away, a heavy clap of thunder shook the house. She winced as she heard an eruption of barking down the hall.

"They're not very fond of storms." Maddie hurried toward the barking. She'd almost made it to the bedroom where the dogs continued to bark, when the lights in the house flickered.

"Maddie." Amber stepped into the hallway. "Did you see the lights?" She rushed toward her.

"I did. The last thing we need is to lose power. Everyone's already so tense. I'm just trying to get to the dogs. I don't trust the water not to get in. I want to make sure they're safe upstairs."

"I'll help you." Amber continued down the hall with her.

Maddie's phone began ringing. "I'm sorry, Amber, it's Jake. I want to get this."

"No problem. I'll round up the dogs." Amber stepped into the bedroom.

Maddie felt some relief as the dogs finally stopped barking. They loved Amber as much as she did.

CHAPTER 17

"Hi, Jake, anything new?" Maddie answered the call.

"Do you have a way out of there?"

"What?" Maddie froze at the sternness in his tone. "You know I don't. The weather is horrible, and in fact, I think we might lose power soon." She watched Pierce walk past her toward the front door.

"I'm going to grab some extra flashlights from my van," Pierce said.

"Be careful!" Maddie watched him go.

"That's what I want you to be. You need to be very cautious. You're under that roof with a murderer, and I can't do anything to help you." Jake's voice was riddled with frustration.

Maddie realized he was worried about her, and everyone there. He had no ability to protect them, and that was his job.

"Jake, when is this rain going to stop?"

"Hopefully, by late morning, but it's going to take some time for the water to recede, so I can get out there. I'm still hoping maybe I can get someone to fly me out there if the weather clears up enough. This is why—" Jake stopped.

Maddie held her breath as she waited for him to finish his statement, to tell her he'd warned her not to go, and she should have listened to him.

"It doesn't matter. I'm sorry. Let's just focus on getting this figured out. Can you send me pictures of everything you found in the attic? I've been looking into Vincent's story. He did have a history of criminal behavior. Things like petty theft and vandalism."

"What about Adam? Did you find out anything more about him?" Maddie asked.

"Adam had several harassment reports made against him, mostly from women he worked with, but the charges have always been dropped. He had a few DUIs also, but again, it seems like he was able to avoid any consequences from them. He seemed like a man who was used to getting away with bad behavior."

"Until now," Maddie whispered. "I guess it caught up with him."

"Hopefully, this will get solved soon, Maddie. Find a weapon to protect yourself with. I'll be there as soon as I can."

"Thanks, Jake." Maddie's muscles tensed as the lights flickered again. She ended the call and slid the phone into her pocket. She wanted to find out who had done this. She was going to do her best to observe everyone there. Hopefully, someone would slip up at some point, and that was going to be the big break. As she opened the bedroom door, Bella and Polly suddenly burst out into the hallway. They ran right past her, straight for the stairs at the end of the hallway.

"Oh no!" Amber raced through the door to chase after them. "I'm so sorry, Maddie!"

"It's okay, don't worry. Those stairs don't lead to anything. They have no way to escape. The storm must have startled them." Maddie started up the stairs after the dogs, then froze at the sight of the empty stairway. "This is impossible. I saw them go up there."

"What do you mean?" Amber ran up behind her. "I saw them, too." She craned her neck to see around Maddie's shoulder. "Where did they go? Did they come back down somehow?"

"No, I would have seen them." Maddie felt a wave of confusion as she continued up the steps. "Bella! Polly! Where are you?"

A sharp bark filled the stairway.

"What's happening?" Maddie looked around her as she heard her dogs bark but didn't see any sign of either of them. "Where are you?"

A few more barks filled the empty space.

"Maddie, I think they're in the wall."

Amber pressed her ear against the wall.

"Yes, the barks are coming from behind there!"

"How?" Maddie leaned her hand against the wall and started to press her ear against it, but before she could, it disappeared. She stumbled through a thin doorway into a small, stuffy, dark space.

"Maddie!" Amber caught her hand as she followed her. "Can you believe this? A hidden door?"

Maddie felt a flood of relief as she crouched down to greet the dogs who eagerly ran up to her. "They must have pushed the door open with their paws." She nestled her nose into the fur of their necks and held them close. "You two gave me such a scare."

"If they didn't, this room sure would." Amber shined the phone's flashlight around the small space. "It's not much bigger than a closet."

"It must be an extra storage space. I guess that's what the stairs actually lead to. But the door was completely hidden." Maddie turned on her own flashlight. "Which is odd. Someone would have to decide to hide it." She lowered the beam of light to a large box in the middle of the small space. "This looks like the only thing in here."

The dogs sniffed and growled at the box.

"Leave it, girls. Let me have a look." Maddie crept closer to the box as the two dogs hung back.

"There's a light switch." Amber flipped it up and down. "But nothing is happening."

"What is this?" Maddie pulled a large gown out of the box. Her eyes widened at the sight of the intricately designed wedding dress. "Is this what I think it is?"

"The Becket bride's dress?" Amber gasped as she looked it over. "Maybe it's been stored here all this time?"

"But didn't she die in this dress? That's what the

legend says." Maddie noticed dirt and what appeared to be a few tears and holes. "Why would anyone keep that?"

"I'm not sure. Look, there's a tag in the box. What does it say on it?" Amber pointed.

"Donovan's." Maddie took a picture of the tag, then looked over the dress again. "If this is her dress, do you know what that means, Amber?"

"That someone has a really terrible sense of sentiment?" Amber scrunched up her nose.

"It means the story is probably true, and there really was a bride in the attic." Maddie glanced around the small alcove again, then looked back at Amber. "But what I don't understand is how it could be hidden here all these years. No one ever found it? Why would it be the only thing stored in here?"

"This house is huge. It's possible no one knew it was here. We didn't know there was a door. Maybe Barbara and her family don't know about it, either."

"But look at the floor." Maddie gestured to the wooden planks. "They aren't covered in dust. I wouldn't look at this space and think it hasn't been touched for decades. Something isn't right about this."

"So, you think Richard and Barbara knew it was

here?" Amber's voice lowered to a whisper. "Maybe they kept it because of some kind of obsession with the Becket bride?"

"Maybe. I think we should leave it here."

"All right." Amber watched Maddie drop the dress back down into the box. "What do you believe?"

"I'm not sure." Maddie recalled the woman she'd seen in the window. Could it really be the same dress? "But I do know a ghost didn't kill Adam. I think a very angry person did that."

"Let's get back to the others before they start wondering where we are and come looking." Amber stepped out of the room and back onto the stairway. "One thing is for sure, this house has far too many secrets. I'm sorry. I never should have convinced you to come here."

Maddie scooped Bella up into her arms and followed Amber, who held Polly, out onto the stairway.

"It's no one's fault we're here. Honestly, I think it's a good thing we are. Maybe we can get to the truth." Maddie descended the stairs right behind Amber. "I just get the feeling everyone is hiding something."

"I think you're right about that." Amber paused at the bottom of the stairs as she watched Debbie cross the hallway in front of her.

CHAPTER 18

"*D*ebbie, are you okay?" Maddie stepped down beside Amber.

Debbie shot Maddie and Amber a dazed look.

"What were you doing up there?"

"We were just getting the dogs. They escaped. Shouldn't you be going upstairs? It's safer up there." Maddie pointed toward the ceiling.

"I was going to go for a smoke first." Debbie patted her pocket. "But I can't find my lighter. I thought I had a spare, but maybe I forgot it at home."

Maddie recalled the lighter she'd found in Adam's coat pocket, but she couldn't tell Debbie that. She might panic and do whatever she could to hide her guilt.

"Can we help you look? It's probably in your room. Don't you think?"

"Sure, maybe. I'm so tired, I can't think straight." Debbie led them to a room a few doors down. "I've been getting my stuff together to move upstairs. I just needed a quick break."

"What does the lighter look like?" Maddie closed the door and set Bella down on the floor next to Polly.

"Small, colorful, with pink flowers." Debbie described the same lighter Maddie had found.

"Maybe it's under the bed." Amber bent down to have a look.

"Let's give the room a good search." Maddie began pulling open drawers, hoping to find something else that might implicate Debbie.

"Ugh, stay away from those." Debbie waved her hands at the dogs as they nuzzled a pile of clothes in the corner of the room.

"Relax, they're not hurting anything." Maddie's quick drive to protect the dogs sharpened her voice.

"I don't want them getting into my stuff. I can look for my lighter on my own, thanks!" Debbie scowled as she watched Amber scoop up Polly. Maddie bent down and picked up Bella.

Maddie froze for a moment as her hands passed

across the damp clothing. She recognized the sweatpants. Debbie had been dressed in them when they first arrived.

"Sure, of course. If we happen to see the lighter anywhere, we'll let you know." Maddie tried to keep her voice even as she stepped into the hallway.

"She's so snappy." Amber shook her head. "Smokers can be that way when they want a cigarette. Try not to take it personally, Maddie."

"I'm not." Maddie lowered her voice as she steered Amber away from the door. "Why don't you see if you can find Tammy, Katie, and your mother. We need to have a discussion. I'll meet you upstairs in the room."

"Okay, I'll round them all up." Amber set off to look for the others.

Soon after Maddie led the dogs into the room, Amber returned with Tammy, Katie, and Iris. She closed the door once they were all inside.

"All right, everyone, it's time to put our heads together." Maddie sat on the edge of the bed as Bella and Polly wrestled playfully by her feet. "I really think Debbie had something to do with Adam's death."

"Are you sure about that?" Iris stared at Maddie. "What makes you believe that?"

"Right now, it's just a hunch, but I think we need to try to find more evidence. I found her lighter in Adam's pocket, and I discovered wet clothes in her room." Maddie glanced around at each of them. "That indicates she was with Adam before he was found dead, and she hasn't admitted to it."

"Wet clothes? We all have piles of wet clothes. Why does that matter?" Tammy asked.

"It matters because the clothes I saw in her room should have been dry. She refused to go outside with Adam while wearing those clothes. Later, straight after I found Adam, I saw her in jeans. Which means she changed her clothes between the time Adam went outside and when I found him." Maddie clasped her hands together. "I know it's a stretch, and maybe there are other explanations, but that, coupled with the lighter in Adam's pocket, points me right in her direction."

"All right, let's play it out." Tammy stood up and strolled back and forth across the room. "We all saw the way Adam spoke to her. Is that really enough to make her want to murder him?"

"She does seem to have a short temper." Iris frowned. "I tried to speak to her a few times, and her answers were sharp and short. She definitely likes her privacy. But then, if she's the killer we're looking for, I guess she wouldn't welcome being questioned."

"Sketchy behavior, on top of everything else. I'm betting there's something there," Katie said.

"Unfortunately, without a little more information, it's not going to be enough. But it's a start." Maddie pulled Bella up into her lap and stroked her back. "Amber and I also found something interesting in a hidden room at the top of the stairs we thought led to nowhere."

"A wedding dress!" Amber jumped to her feet. "All torn and dirty. It was the only thing hidden in that little room. We think it might have been the Becket bride's dress."

"Really?" Tammy gasped. "Barbara told me a bit more about that story. She's pretty convinced the bride's ghost really is haunting this house."

"I thought the story of the Becket bride was probably just a story, but maybe it is based on some fact," Iris said.

"I'm going to look into the history of this house. We need some clear answers." Katie sat down on the bed with her phone and began searching. "It shouldn't take me too long to come up with something."

"Katie, while you're looking into the house, I'm

going to look into Vincent and see if I can find out more about him." Maddie let the dog jump down from her lap.

"You two do that. I want to have a look at that dress myself." Iris walked toward the door.

"Not alone you won't." Amber followed her.

"What happened to that speech you gave me about being a grown woman able to make her own choices?" Iris raised her eyebrows.

"This is different." Amber wrapped her arm around Iris. "You're my mother. I can't let anything happen to you."

"Very sweet." Tammy grinned. "Maybe I should go with you to keep you both out of trouble."

"Good luck with that." Maddie laughed. "But do stick together and be careful."

"We will." Tammy followed them out into the hallway.

"I found something interesting." Katie held her phone out to Maddie. "Or actually, it's more about what I can't find. There's no record of anyone else dying on this property, other than Vincent."

"Nothing about the Becket bride? Are you sure?" Maddie asked.

"There are rumors about it, people theorizing about the legend. But no actual proof the bride ever existed." Katie looked up from her phone at Maddie. "Vincent's death barely got a mention. Just a few articles about people claiming to see the ghost of the bride on the roof with him. Do you remember it? What about you, Mom?" She glanced over at her mother as she, Amber, and Iris filed back into the room.

"No, I can't say that I do. But that wedding dress is weird. I'm not sure what to think about it. Do you remember anything about Vincent dying, Maddie?" Tammy asked.

"No, I would have only been about eight at the time," Maddie said.

"I do remember when it happened." Iris sat down on a wooden chair beside a small table.

"Did you know Richard and Barbara at that time?" Maddie walked over to her. "Do you remember any rumors that might have been flying around town?"

"Just the rumors about the ghost. The B&B opening had caused so much excitement in the area. We were looking forward to the additional tourists Becket House would bring in." Iris clasped her hands together. "I knew them at school, but they were a few years older than me. I didn't know them very well. They were high school sweethearts and have always been very close. Vincent was new to town, and it wasn't long after he moved here that he died. Like I said, I assumed Vincent had fallen off the roof, and the stories about the ghost being up there with him were just that, stories."

"Exactly." Maddie looked up as the overhead light in the room began to flicker.

CHAPTER 19

"*I* think we need to stay focused on the present, not the past." Tammy sat down on the bed with Polly. "A few things point to Debbie. She worked with him. Maybe he did something more than just ridicule her in front of others."

"Maybe. Alexandra did tell me that Adam tried to kiss her and pressure her into going out with him behind Silla's back. Now that I think about it, Alexandra is probably the person I should be talking to. Silla and Adam were only together for a short time, but Alexandra and Adam had a history. I'm going to see if I can get her to talk to me a little more. I think she'll be more open with me if I'm alone." As Maddie walked toward the door, she glanced back at the others. "The rest of you, sit tight. I don't want to have to worry about any of you getting hurt. The lights are barely hanging on, and we still have no idea who really did this." She started to open the door.

"That's all the more reason for us to help." Katie jumped to her feet. "We can talk to everyone again."

"No." Maddie turned toward her. "It's late. Everyone's tired. Let them rest a little, then we might get more out of them after."

"She's right." Tammy slung her arm around her daughter's shoulders. "We're better off sticking together if the lights might go out. Maddie, don't be gone for long, okay?"

"I won't be." Maddie stepped out into the hall and made her way toward the top of the stairs. As she reached them, she spotted Pierce on the other side of the hallway about to step into one of the rooms. "Pierce." She waved to get his attention. He turned around to face her. "Sorry, I just wanted to know if you've seen Alexandra."

"Here I am." Alexandra walked up behind Maddie from the top of the stairs as Pierce stepped into the room and closed the door.

"Oh, I wanted to speak to you." Maddie turned around to face her.

"What is it?" Alexandra walked toward the room next to Pierce's and opened the door. "I'm really tired."

"I know you must be." Maddie crossed the distance between them. "I just need to speak to you for a minute."

"Oh, have you figured out who killed Adam?" Alexandra stepped into the room and gestured for Maddie to join her. "You can tell me. I'll keep quiet about it."

"Unfortunately, I haven't figured that out just yet. Is there anything else you can tell me about him? I wish I had more insight into his life," Maddie said.

"Has his phone been found?" Alexandra leaned against the wall just inside the door and stared across the space at the window that overlooked the driveway below.

"No, unfortunately not. I think there's a good chance it was swept away in the floodwaters." Maddie looked in her direction. What was that heaviness in her eyes? Grief? Fear? Something in between?

"But you don't know that, do you?" Alexandra frowned and shifted her gaze toward the front hallway. "It's an important piece of evidence. I'll go look for it as soon as the storm subsides."

"Alexandra, is there something you're not telling me?" Maddie straightened up and walked over to her. "What's on his phone that's so important to you?"

"You're so paranoid." Alexandra rolled her eyes. "Just because your police chief friend gave you an imaginary badge, that doesn't make you good at this. I'm trying to help."

"See, that's what I mean." Maddie studied her expression. "You're so angry. I get it, after the way he treated you. But you went out there to get your job back, didn't you?"

"Yes." Alexandra lowered her eyes as her cheeks flushed.

"Did you see Debbie out there? Was she with him?"

"I didn't see anyone. I told you that already. The only person I saw was you." Alexandra stared straight at her. "You were outside around the time he was killed, weren't you? You could have killed him just as easily as any of the rest of us."

"But I had no reason to. I didn't even know Adam. From what I've learned about him, he wasn't the easiest man to get along with."

Alexandra snorted and smirked. "That's an understatement."

"Is it? Why?" Maddie searched her eyes. "We need the murder solved as soon as possible. We need the people who really knew Adam to help try to get to the bottom of this. I know he hurt you. What really happened after you rejected him? You don't seem like the type of person who would suddenly surrender to someone like that. You strike me as so strong and determined. Why would you want to work with him again after what he did to you?"

"I didn't have a choice," Alexandra snapped.

"What do you mean?"

"If I tell you, you'll only think I killed him." Alexandra cleared her throat. "I can't go to prison for something I didn't do."

"Listen, you're right, I'm not really a detective. That means I'm not obligated to follow the rules like a real police officer. I can just listen. I can hear your whole story, and we can decide together what's important to share and what isn't. I know this is about more than your career. What really happened?"

"When I turned him down, he was angry. He said I was being difficult. I asked him about Silla.

Didn't he even care about hurting her that way? He insisted that he didn't care about her, that she had connections that he needed to get the show made." Alexandra's upper lip curled with disgust. "Clearly, she's in love with him, though." She took a deep breath. "When I rejected him and told him that I quit, I wouldn't be working for him, he got even angrier. He said he wouldn't force me to go out with him but that I couldn't abandon the show because it would ruin everything. So, he threatened me."

"How?" Maddie asked.

"He threatened to release a really embarrassing video of me when I was drunk. I said things I never should have. If it got out, it would end my career. At first I told him I didn't care, to just release it. But after I thought about it, I changed my mind. That's why I went out there to find him. I decided I would do the job if he would promise to delete the video. Now, I have no idea where the video is." Alexandra held out her hands, palms up. "And there it is, that look in your eyes. I know what you're thinking. Maybe you think I did kill him. But I didn't. You have to believe me, Maddie. You do believe me, don't you?"

"Yes, of course I do. But you have to help me figure out who really did this. It's the only way to keep your name clear." Maddie didn't know whether to believe Alexandra was innocent, but if she pretended she did, Alexandra might let something slip.

"I didn't want to say anything because, really, he deserved it, but I'm sure it was Silla. I didn't feel right about anything that happened. So, I went to her and told her what he did. I heard them arguing not long after. I'm sure the whole house heard them," Alexandra said.

Maddie recalled Silla saying she had spent time having a relaxing lunch with Adam earlier in the day.

"You're sure they were arguing?"

"Yes. I heard them arguing, but I couldn't really hear what it was about. Then I heard something crash." Alexandra frowned. "Maybe I shouldn't have said anything at all. I might not have drowned him, but if she did it, maybe I'm to blame."

"You did the right thing by telling her the truth. You were trying to protect her." Maddie patted her arm. "Try to get some rest."

As Maddie stepped out of the room, her thoughts shifted to Silla. If Alexandra had told her the truth, then Silla had told her a lie.

CHAPTER 20

*P*ierce rushed out of the room next to Alexandra's.

"Pierce? What's wrong? Why are you in such a hurry?" Maddie turned around as he passed her.

"I need to get some extra equipment. If the lights go out, I'm sure I'll catch some paranormal activity. I just need to make sure everything is set up right." Pierce rubbed the bruise on his face. "And hopefully, I won't drop another camera on myself."

"Be careful. With the way this storm is raging, I wouldn't be surprised if it causes some damage to the house."

"Oh, this old girl has withstood many storms." Pierce disappeared down the stairs.

Maddie lingered for a moment, considering

whether to follow and ask him more about his relationship with Adam.

"I doubt he'll share anything more with me," Maddie muttered to herself. She swept her gaze along the rooms on the second-floor hallway. She had no idea which one Silla might be in. Resigned to knocking on each door, she walked to the next room. Before she could knock, she noticed Silla curled up in a large easy chair positioned beside a tall window that overlooked the rear of the property.

"Silla?" Maddie paused next to the chair and noted the paleness of the woman's skin. "Are you all right?"

"I was just thinking of him." Silla stared down at her folded hands.

"I'm so sorry, Silla. This must be so hard for you."

"Hard is not the word I would use to describe it. Unreal, impossible." Silla stood up and turned toward the window. "I just want all of this to have been a terrible dream."

"At least you had some beautiful memories with him, right?" Maddie watched her, searching for the sign that would indicate her deceit. "You had a nice lunch together, didn't you?"

"Yes, of course. We had many special moments." Silla continued to stare through the window. "But that doesn't exactly comfort me. It feels like my heart has been ripped out and stomped all over. I wonder if I'll ever be able to love again."

"Maybe your heart didn't start feeling that way when he died." Maddie took a step closer as she braced herself for Silla's reaction. "Maybe it started feeling that way when Alexandra told you what he did."

Silla spun around to face Maddie.

"She told you?" Silla's voice trembled with anger. "She couldn't keep her lying mouth shut for two seconds? That doesn't surprise me."

"You think she was lying? You don't think Adam tried to go out with her behind your back?"

"Why would he ever?" Silla gestured to her slim figure. "Look at me! I'm gorgeous!"

"I can see that." Maddie wondered what it would feel like to have so much confidence. Or was it arrogance? "But being beautiful doesn't stop a cheater from cheating. It's just something they do. And he planned on doing it to you, Silla. Which must have made you very angry. You argued, didn't you?"

"Yes, we argued," Silla snapped. "Of course we

did. After Alexandra fed me those lies, I was upset. Who wouldn't be? So, I let him know exactly how I expect to be treated. That's when he told me he planned to propose to me. That's why he had brought me here. He thought it would be nice to pop the question at a place I wouldn't expect. It would come as a complete surprise. He said Alexandra was just jealous. He had asked her to come here because he thought she could use the work, but she's the one who made a pass at him. When he told her he only wanted to be with me, she threatened to quit. Can you believe that? It would have ruined the show. It would have been impossible for Adam to find a replacement at such short notice." She rolled her eyes. "She must be so desperate."

"I'm not sure what to believe." Maddie raised her eyebrows. "I think Adam could have been lying to you."

"He wouldn't." Silla bit into her bottom lip. "Like I said, he planned to propose."

"Then where's the ring? If he planned to propose, he would have had the ring with him, right? Did you find it in his room? In his things? Did he tell you where it was?"

"No." Silla sniffled as she looked back down at

her hands. "He probably had it in his pocket. Maybe he lost it in the water when that awful person murdered my sweet Adam."

Maddie didn't want to upset Silla anymore. Yes, Silla had lied to her, and she might be lying to her again. But if she didn't kill Adam, then she'd lost him, right when she thought their relationship might be going to the next level.

"Just leave me alone. I want to be alone. I can't stand being here a moment longer, knowing that he's gone forever. But I don't have a choice because we're all stuck in this horrible place. So, please, just leave me alone."

"Okay, Silla." Maddie backed up toward the stairway. "But please let me know if you need anything."

As Maddie passed the stairs, lightning illuminated their grand slope. For an instant, she thought she saw someone at the base of them, looking up at her. But after blinking, the silhouette disappeared. Her heart raced as she hurried back to the room. Her imagination was obviously getting away from her yet again.

CHAPTER 21

*M*addie pushed the door to the room open and stepped inside. As she closed the door behind her, Polly and Bella rushed toward her with eager barks. She could see the excitement in the way they bounced from paw to paw and lapped at her hands.

"Hi, girls." Maddie gave them each a kiss before she looked up at the others. "I need to run through something with you."

"What is it?" Tammy leaned forward slightly.

"It's just that I have plenty of reason to believe that Debbie, or Silla, or even Pierce could have been involved in Adam's murder, but I have no real evidence on any of them. Now Silla has told me

Alexandra is the liar, and Adam had planned to propose to Silla." Maddie ran her hands along the dogs' backs. "She insists that Alexandra is the one who made a move on Adam, not the other way around. Which, of course, gives Silla less of a motive to kill Adam."

"So, who do we believe?" Amber asked.

"Well, Silla definitely lied to you, Maddie, right?" Iris tapped her fingers against the bed. "She claimed she had a relaxed lunch with Adam, but that wasn't the truth, was it?"

"No, Silla admitted they did argue. I guess she felt embarrassed, or didn't want to look guilty, and decided to cover it up. But she did tell me they argued about Alexandra, and that's when Adam told her he planned to propose to her. But she doesn't have the ring. Apparently, it isn't in his things, and it wasn't in his coat pockets. I guess it could be lost in the water. But she could be lying to me, or he could have been lying to her," Maddie said.

"Either way, it doesn't explain why he's dead." Tammy sank into her chair. "All it does is make more of the witnesses unreliable."

"Yes, exactly." Maddie sat beside Tammy. "That's the problem. As I said, we don't have any real evidence."

"You're right. We just found those old light bulbs and trash outside. No sign of what actually happened to Adam," Katie said.

"Wait, there is something else." Maddie gasped. "I can't believe I forgot about it." She slid her hand into her pocket. "The paper we found in Adam's pocket. It should be dry by now. Maybe it has something to do with him proposing to Silla. It could at least confirm her story."

Maddie began to carefully unfold the paper as the others drew close and watched. She quickly realized there were two pieces. One was thick and square, the other thin and rectangular, and part of it was torn off. They both were handwritten.

"The thin and torn piece is completely faded and illegible. It looks very old. The other one looks just as old. It doesn't look like it has anything to do with a proposal, either, but it does have something to do with a wedding dress." Maddie assessed the information on the thick paper. "It's a receipt, from a long time ago. The ink has smudged a lot, and I can't quite make out the name of the store, but part of the date is clear. Almost forty years ago, someone purchased a wedding dress."

"Why would Adam have a receipt for a forty-year-old wedding dress in his pocket?" Tammy shook her head. "That doesn't make any sense."

"Maybe it doesn't, but he probably had it for a reason. We just need to figure out what." Maddie stared at the paper. "It's obviously not his. He wasn't even forty years old. So, where did he get it from?"

"Do you think it has something to do with the wedding dress we found?" Amber peered closer at the receipt.

"I'm not sure. But if it does, if it's a receipt for that dress, then it's clear the dress didn't belong to the Becket bride. She died long before that. About a hundred years ago. Didn't she?" Maddie looked at the others, who nodded in agreement.

"If she even existed, which we still haven't proven." Tammy pursed her lips.

"I can confirm the dress you found can't be the Becket bride's dress." Katie looked up from her phone. "I looked up the name of the store that was on the tag in the box, and it only opened for business fifty years ago. The bride died years before that. From what I can tell, it looks like this receipt is from the same place. So, there's a good chance the receipt is for that dress and zero chance it belongs to the Becket bride."

"All right, maybe Barbara or Richard can offer

more information about the dress since it's quite old." Maddie handed the receipts over to Katie. "Can you take some good pictures of these and send them to Jake for me, please? The techs at the station might be able to find out more about them."

"Sure, I'll do that." Katie took the receipts and set them out on the bed next to her to take some pictures.

"I'll go with you to speak to them. I don't want them teaming up against you." Amber grinned at Maddie.

"Okay, thanks. But I want to take Polly and Bella outside first." Maddie grabbed their leashes.

"I'll come with you." Amber stepped out into the hall and walked with Maddie and the dogs outside. "At least the storm has died down a bit."

"Yes." Maddie tightened her coat around herself. She was pleased the dogs were eager to get back inside. They didn't take long or wander far before they started to pull back toward the front door.

After Maddie and Amber settled Bella and Polly in the room, they stepped back out into the hallway.

"Let's try to find Richard and Barbara." Maddie tipped her head toward the stairway. "I'm pretty sure they're on the third floor."

"All right, let's see what they have to say. I really

hope they have a logical explanation for the dress being in that room."

"I'm not sure what it could be." Maddie led the way up the stairs to the third floor.

"Let's find out." Amber pointed out Barbara who had just stepped into the third-floor hallway.

CHAPTER 22

"*B*arbara! We need to speak with you, please." Maddie hurried down the hall before Barbara could disappear back inside the room.

"Sure." Barbara glanced at the two of them. "Shh! Quiet, please. Richard is resting." She stepped out into the hall and closed the door behind her. "What has you all upset? Other than the great flood out there." She wrung her hands as she looked down the stairway in the direction of the front door. "There's definitely water gathering down there."

"The storm isn't what has me worried right now." Maddie stepped into Barbara's line of sight. "I have a couple of questions for you."

"Sure." Barbara looked past Maddie, at Amber, then back at Maddie. "What's going on here?"

"We found a secret room." Maddie noticed a flicker of recognition in Barbara's expression.

"So, you've been snooping around the house after how kind we've been to all of you?" Barbara clucked her tongue. "That doesn't seem very neighborly of you."

"We weren't snooping. We were looking for the dogs. They were startled by the storm and escaped. When we went after them, we found a wedding dress that you have hidden in that secret room at the top of the stairs," Maddie said.

Barbara stared at her for a long moment. Her lips moved as if she was searching for the right words to say, then she laughed.

"Oh, is that all this is about? Yes, I know about the dress."

"You don't just know about it, do you?" Maddie crossed her arms. "You bought the dress."

"Sure, yes, I bought it." Barbara nodded. "It's my wedding dress. I wore it on the best day of my life. When I married my Richard."

"You did?" Maddie narrowed her eyes. "But why is it all torn?"

"That's Cynthia's doing." Barbara smiled

wistfully. "I gave it to her, and she wore it when she married Dirk. She accidently got it caught on the car door when she was coming home from the reception. It ripped, and she obviously doesn't need it anymore, so she decided not to get it repaired. She wanted to wear it for Halloween. I thought, why not. It's so old now anyway. But with everything that's happened, we haven't gotten round to wearing costumes."

"And the secret room?" Maddie asked.

"It's not a secret. We always meant to do something with that room and that side of the house, but we didn't get around to it. But you know kids." Barbara waved her hand through the air. "Full of energy and grand ideas. Dirk and Cynthia have been cleaning out everything and reorganizing things. They're going to use it as a storage room and do some renovating in that area."

"Okay." Maddie felt a bit foolish that she thought something nefarious was going on with the dress. "And you really didn't mind Cynthia wearing your wedding dress as a Halloween costume?"

"No, I've run a haunted B&B for years, and now the grandkids are running it. I want the best for them, and costumes and other things like that can only help them run a successful haunted house.

When you run a haunted house, guests have certain expectations. People pay top dollar for the experience," Barbara said.

Maddie hesitated before she asked the next question. She had no real evidence to implicate Dirk or Cynthia, aside from Alexandra mentioning she had overheard them having some sort of argument about the documentary, which they'd brushed off, but she wanted to see what Barbara had to say.

"Do you think it's possible Dirk or Cynthia could have had something to do with Adam's murder?" Maddie watched the anger cross Barbara's face. "Someone heard them arguing about Adam and the documentary."

"Wait just a second." Barbara scowled. "My family has been very generous by providing everyone with a place to stay during the storm. I won't have them accused like that, young lady!" Her gaze sharpened.

Maddie choked back a laugh at being called "young lady" and tried to stay focused.

"We appreciate your hospitality. I'm not accusing anyone. We just want to find out the truth." Maddie looked straight into her eyes.

"That's all very well, but I'll thank you to keep

your manners while you're staying under my roof," Barbara snapped.

"What's going on here? Is everything okay?" Cynthia walked down the hallway.

"Yes, just a misunderstanding. Maddie came across the wedding dress." Barbara smiled.

"Oh, my Halloween costume." Cynthia sighed. "If only I had the chance to wear it."

"Maddie is still trying to find out the truth about who the murderer is," Barbara said.

"Oh, I can understand that. If there's someone you should suspect, it's that Pierce fellow. If you want truth, I'll tell you some about him. He came and told us how he wanted to make a documentary about the house and how it was haunted. He seemed so passionate about telling the story of the ghosts that inhabit it," Cynthia said.

"Dirk liked how passionate he was about it, so against our better judgment, they agreed to let Pierce come here to film." Barbara glanced at Cynthia. "Then Adam showed up. He told us Pierce has a record, a history of violence. He warned us that we shouldn't let Pierce produce the documentary, as if the truth came out about Pierce's past, it might put a cloud on the whole show."

"So, that's why we let Adam take over filming

here and put him in touch with Vincent's family."
Cynthia stepped toward Maddie as her voice grew
stern. "There's your truth."

"If you want to throw around accusations, go
find Pierce," Barbara said.

"It isn't my intention to upset any of you. Why
wouldn't you mention this information about Pierce
before? Were you trying to protect him?" Maddie
asked.

"No. I asked Barbara and Richard not to
mention anything." Cynthia bit her bottom lip.
"After Adam died, we knew we were going to lose
out on the publicity from the documentary. When
Pierce said he would still film it, we decided to keep
our mouths shut, and we asked Barbara and
Richard to do the same. We're going to lose a lot of
potential money if the show doesn't get aired."

"Look, I've had enough of these questions. I
have nothing else to say to you. If you want to ask
me or my family more questions, you'll have to get
the real cops out here to do it." Barbara grabbed
Cynthia's hand and pulled her down the hallway
and into a room.

The sharp snap of the door closing made
Cynthia and Barbara's message very clear.

CHAPTER 23

*M*addie looked from the closed door over at Amber.

"I guess Barbara and Cynthia are done talking with us," Maddie said.

"Yes, it looks like our imaginations got away with us about what the wedding dress was doing in that room. Wait, do you think it was Cynthia in the attic window earlier? Maybe she was wearing the dress."

"Maybe. But I thought the person in the window had blonde hair, and surely she would have mentioned it." Maddie started down the stairs. "We need to speak to Pierce. If we believe what Cynthia said, he's been hiding the truth about his past."

"And Adam really threw him under the bus by

159

telling Cynthia and Dirk the truth about it." Amber followed her down the stairs back to the second floor. "That's a pretty strong motive to want to get revenge on Adam."

"Yes, it is. So, I'm going to speak with him again. Can you please let the others know what we found out about the dress?"

"Sure." Amber smiled.

Maddie looked at her phone as it beeped. "Oh, it's from Jake. It says to be cautious of Pierce." She looked up at Amber. "He probably found out he has a criminal history."

"Looks like Cynthia was telling the truth about him," Amber said.

"Can you update Jake for me, about what Cynthia said about Pierce's past, please? He might be able to put something more together if he knows Adam told Cynthia and the others about it. Let him know what we've found out so far." Maddie paused at the landing for the second floor. "But don't tell him I'm going to talk to Pierce alone."

"Why? Because he would tell you it's a foolish choice?" Amber stared hard into her eyes. "Why do you want to meet with him alone? He could be a killer, Maddie. You should have someone there with you."

"Pierce is already on the defensive from our last conversation. I need him to be as relaxed as possible, if there's any chance of him talking to me. Just trust me on this one, okay, Amber?" Maddie held her gaze.

"All right, I'll trust you. Just don't make me regret it."

"I won't. I promise." Maddie smiled at her before she continued down the stairs toward the first floor.

With Pierce determined to get some recordings for his show, Maddie doubted he would be hidden away in any of the upstairs rooms. A faint light glowed inside the dining room. As she crept closer to the doorway, she tried to prepare herself for how Pierce might react to what she had to say. Already, she'd seen him get pretty volatile when confronted. She paused in the doorway and peered inside.

"Pierce?"

"Shh!" Pierce stepped out of a shadowy corner. "I'm recording."

"Sorry," Maddie whispered and watched as he pushed some buttons on his equipment.

"There." Pierce glanced up at her. "It's all right, I wasn't getting much other than thunder. I keep hoping someone will want to talk to me, or at least make some sounds, but I'm not getting much. I was really hoping Vincent would tell me what happened to him."

"You're very passionate about finding out more about the ghosts in this house, aren't you?"

"Yes."

"So, what do you think happened to Vincent? I'm sure you've done plenty of research, so what do your instincts tell you?" Maddie stepped farther into the dining room.

"I think he was somehow killed by the ghost of the Becket bride, but something else was going on in his life at the time. I think he went to the police just a few days before he died. But I can't find an official report, so they couldn't confirm it and tell me why." Pierce sighed.

"He did have a bit of a past, didn't he? A few run-ins with the law?" Maddie watched as he looked back at her. "Not unlike you."

Pierce's expression grew tense. "What are you talking about?"

"I know about your history, Pierce," Maddie said.

"So, I got into a little bit of trouble when I was younger. Who didn't?" Pierce scowled. "It was nothing. I went through my rebellious phase. I stole a few cars. Got into a few fights. Nothing that was that big a deal. But I got arrested a few times. I thought maybe if I tried hard enough, I would be cool enough to get the girl. But it never worked." He shrugged. "So, I left my past behind and turned over a new leaf. The only problem is the past didn't let go of me. Every time I go for a job interview, I have to tell them about that. And every time, I get the same response. It doesn't matter how many good things I've done since then, all that matters is that record, which follows me around. That's why I had to strike out on my own. I needed to create my own business because it was the only way I could get anywhere in life. When I saw this opportunity, I knew I had to take it. Then Adam swooped in and took it out from under me."

"Literally. Cynthia told me she and Dirk decided to let him take over after he told them about your history." Maddie settled her gaze on him. "But you knew that, didn't you? Isn't that why you decided to go out into the rain after him?"

"No." Pierce glared at her. "Don't even start that nonsense. I had nothing to do with Adam's death, and nothing you say will change that."

"It's not about what I say. I don't know what happened to Adam. But I do know you had to be incredibly angry at him, and that anger has to go somewhere. It doesn't just disappear." Maddie took a slight step back as he shifted closer to her with fury in his eyes.

"I might have been angry, but I didn't kill him!"

Suddenly, the entire house plunged into complete darkness.

A crash above their heads inspired a shriek from the opposite corner of the dining room and a gasp from Pierce.

Maddie flinched as she saw Debbie jump to her feet. She hadn't seen her sitting there the whole time.

"Debbie, hurry! We need to get this on film!" Pierce called out. "Bring the camera. It's him. It's Vincent."

In the jumble of flashlight beams, Maddie watched Debbie bolt for the door and head off down the hallway in the opposite direction from Pierce.

CHAPTER 24

A sudden lightning flash sent the dining room from pitch blackness into a garish bright light.

As it did, Maddie noticed something on a nearby shelf. A photograph. Actually, a group of photographs. But only one held her attention.

As she stared at the image, a loud crash of thunder inspired scattered gasps and shrieks from all different directions. Some came from upstairs, others from dark hallways. Despite the chaos, her gaze remained locked on the photograph as her mind tried to process what it meant.

Maddie pulled out her phone and snapped a picture of the photograph, which featured a much younger Barbara and Richard on their wedding day.

As she took a step back, her foot slid across the floor with something slippery wedged underneath it. She caught her balance and reached down to pick up what turned out to be a cell phone. She recognized the pattern on the phone case. It matched the pattern on the lighter she'd found in Adam's pocket. As she stared down at the still open screen, she read a text that appeared Debbie had been in the middle of deleting.

If he mouths off to me one more time, I'm going to make sure that he never has another thing to say.

A quick scan of the previous texts indicated the conversation had been between Debbie and a friend, and the topic had been Adam.

Maddie read over the words again and again. She'd been focused on Pierce as the best potential suspect, but now she had to wonder if Debbie had done it. Had she been pushed to the edge by Adam? She'd worked with someone she didn't respect or like. She didn't doubt Debbie had enough spunk and strength to pull it off.

Debbie had run out of the room. Was it because she thought Maddie had figured something out? She held her breath as another roll of thunder rattled the house. She thought about Bella and Polly and hoped they were okay. They weren't too bad in storms, but she still wanted to be with them. A flurry of movement outside the dining room caught Maddie's attention.

In the flickering light and the thunder to punctuate her every thought, Maddie knew what she had to do. She needed to get the truth from Debbie. She needed to find out if she had killed Adam.

Maddie stepped out into the dark hallway outside the dining room. A quick flick of her wrist turned on the flashlight on her phone. She aimed it in both directions, up and down the hall. It was empty. She still had no idea what the crash had been. But she knew she had to find out and make sure everyone in the house was safe. Had the killer taken advantage of the blackout and decided to get rid of someone else?

Maddie noticed a flashlight beam at the end of the hallway before the person who held it came into view.

"Cynthia, are you okay?"

"Yes, and you?"

"I'm fine," Maddie said.

"I'm just going to go upstairs and check on the others. Dirk is already up there."

"Okay, I'll be up there soon."

Maddie started down the hallway as Cynthia walked up the stairs. Maddie wanted to try to find Debbie.

"Hello?" Maddie called out. She could hear the steady rain, which was only interrupted by the rumble of thunder. A faint sound from inside the closet at the end of the hall caught her attention. This time, she didn't call out. She didn't want to alert whoever might be inside to the fact she had heard something.

A few more quiet steps placed Maddie right in front of the partially open closet door. She held her breath, determined not to give away her presence. As she reached for the doorknob, her hand trembled. What would happen once she opened the door? Would someone jump out at her, ready to attack?

Maddie grasped the knob, and in one quick movement she swung the door open and held her breath at the same time. The sight of Debbie standing inside the closet shocked her.

"Debbie. What are you doing in there?" Maddie pointed her flashlight directly at her.

"Hiding." Debbie cringed. "I was just hiding out so Pierce couldn't find me. He wants me to keep filming, and this place is freaking me out. I just need a break. I need to sort out everything in my mind."

"You dropped your phone." Maddie handed her phone over.

"Oh, I didn't realize." Debbie touched her pocket. "It must have been on my lap and fallen off when I stood up."

"I noticed some messages on there, when I was trying to work out who the phone belonged to."

"Oh no. I feel terrible about what I wrote." Debbie stepped out of the closet. "I said some things I shouldn't have before Adam died. Of course, if I had known someone was going to kill him, I wouldn't have sent those messages or posted all of those rants about him. Now I look like a very cold and cruel person." She cringed. "But that wasn't my intention. I just wanted to get the truth about him out there."

"And what truth is that?" Maddie lowered the light but continued to block the closet doorway. "What did you think everyone needed to know about Adam?"

"Adam was a liar. He took advantage of everyone he worked with. When I overheard him and Alexandra arguing, it made me so angry. That's why I went out after him. I wanted to give him a piece of my mind and warn him I would be telling everyone." Debbie leaned against the wall and closed her eyes. "But I lost my nerve. I found him standing over this pile of garbage, and he screamed at me to get my camera to film it. That's when I gave him my lighter. He was trying to see what was written on the side of one of the lights, and he didn't have his phone."

"Why didn't he have his phone? Did he say?"

"He accidently dropped it in the water. He was going to go in after it, but first he wanted me to take pictures of the garbage. I refused to do it. I couldn't bring myself to tell him what I knew about his argument with Alexandra, but I wasn't about to ruin my camera by bringing it out into the rain, either." Debbie lowered her eyes. "He was so angry at me. He kept shouting about it being the most important part of the documentary and how I was going to ruin everything. He wouldn't let me say a single word, he just kept shouting at me. That's when I'd had enough and realized I would never get through to him. So, I left." She looked back up at Maddie. "I can't say I didn't think about hurting him. He annoyed me so much. Made me so angry. But I didn't hurt him. I didn't act on it. I walked away." She shrugged. "I can't prove that to you, but it's the truth." She looked up as the lights flickered back on.

"That's good, at least." Maddie turned off her flashlight. "Get somewhere safe, and stay there. Okay? Things are really chaotic, and I still don't know what caused that crash."

"I'm going back upstairs." Debbie brushed past her and headed toward the stairs. At the bottom of them she looked back at Maddie. "I didn't do it, Maddie. I swear. I know you might not believe me, but I'm telling the truth."

"Just stay safe. We can figure out the rest later." Maddie swept her gaze along the hallway as she wondered where Pierce had gone. Before she could begin to search for him, her cell phone rang. The moment she saw Jake's name, she answered it. "Jake."

"I was able to make out more of the writing on the photos of the receipts Katie sent to me." Jake's voice kept breaking up as the storm continued to rage.

"What?" Maddie pressed the phone harder against her ear, though she knew it would make no difference. "Jake, I can barely hear you. You're breaking up." The line went dead.

Maddie looked at her cell phone.

"No reception," she muttered as she walked down the hallway. Maybe she would find reception in a different area of the house. She continued down the hallway and tried to call Jake back, but there was still no cell phone service. As she walked past a room, she noticed the door was slightly open. She peered through the crack into the small office. She noticed a few framed newspaper articles on the walls from years before. They were about the house and how it was haunted. She walked inside and scanned over them. Nothing caught her attention in particular.

As Maddie turned to leave, she glanced down at the desk. There was one piece of paper on it. It was a printout of an email. Maddie could see it was only sent a few hours before Adam's death. It was between Cynthia and what looked like a lawyer. Cynthia wanted to know if there was any way she could get out of the contract with Adam and exactly what he could and couldn't report on. The lawyer advised the contract they had signed meant Adam had free reign, and it would be very difficult if not impossible to get out of.

Maddie's heart raced as everything fell into place. Cynthia must have killed Adam to stop him from filming. Or was it both Cynthia and Dirk? But why? Maybe the argument Alexandra claimed to overhear between Cynthia and Dirk about the documentary was about getting out of the contract. Maybe Adam discovered something about the B&B, and he was going to reveal it in his show. Something Dirk and Cynthia didn't want exposed. But what was it?

Maddie's thoughts shifted to the promise Cynthia had made earlier. She'd gone upstairs to join Dirk to check on everyone. Her friends and family were all alone in that small room and had no idea that it was likely Cynthia and Dirk who were the murderers. They had no idea they might be in danger from them.

Without a second thought, Maddie charged up the stairs to the second floor.

CHAPTER 25

s Maddie reached the hallway of the second floor, she found chaos. Several vases and tables had been knocked over, and Amber and Katie were running in opposite directions up and down the hall, calling for Polly and Bella.

"What happened?" Maddie searched for any sign of her dogs.

"I'm so sorry, Aunt Maddie," Katie gasped. "When the lights went out, I opened the door. I couldn't see the dogs, and they got away from me. I tried to catch them, but I crashed into things in the darkness, and they took off. We've been looking for them, but we don't know where they went."

"I don't think they're on the second floor with us anymore," Amber said.

"Okay, it's all right, don't panic. They can't get outside. They're going to be fine. We just need to find them." Maddie tried to keep calm. "We're going to have to split up." She nodded at Tammy and Iris as they joined them in the hallway. "We have two missions. We need to find Polly and Bella, but we also need to make sure Cynthia and Dirk can't hurt anyone else. I'm pretty sure they're the ones who killed Adam."

"Seriously?" Tammy stared at her with wide eyes. "What makes you think that?"

"I don't have time to explain, but please, if you run into them, keep your distance. If they're worried about being caught, they might be ruthless and desperate. I'm going to go upstairs to speak to them right now." Maddie looked up in the direction of the third floor. "Hopefully, I'll find the dogs on the way."

"Cynthia and Dirk aren't up there. After they checked on us, they said they would be checking on things on the first floor." Katie's voice took on a higher pitch.

"All right, I'm going that way, then. Everyone stay with someone else. Don't be alone." Maddie started down the stairs.

"That includes you, Aunt Maddie." Katie followed her.

"Mom and I will search upstairs." Amber and Iris started up the stairway to the third floor.

"Where Katie goes, I'm going." Tammy joined them on their descent to the first floor.

"I'm so sorry, again, Aunt Maddie. They just bolted," Katie fretted as she followed Maddie.

"Don't worry, Katie. Bella and Polly are tough little pups. They'll find a dry place to hide and will be well-rested by the time we find them. I don't trust Cynthia and Dirk not to try to escape or hurt someone else." Maddie reached the first floor and stepped down into a few inches of water. "Wow, it really is getting more flooded by the moment."

"I hear someone talking in the kitchen." Katie tipped her head toward it.

"And I said all we have to do is get on a boat and get out of here." Richard's angry voice carried into the hallway.

"We have to wait," Barbara replied.

"It's Richard and Barbara," Maddie whispered. "Sounds like they want to leave."

"You listen in, and I'll keep looking for the pups." Tammy hurried off down the hallway.

As Maddie walked toward the kitchen, her

phone vibrated. She looked at a text which was from Jake.

It explained the other receipt was for a wig and makeup. Everything, including the wedding dress, was bought on the same day in early May, a month before Vincent died. She remembered the photo of Richard and Barbara on their wedding day. As she did, everything finally fell into place.

Maddie's mind spun at the realization.

"What if the Becket bride really did kill Vincent?" she murmured to herself.

"What, you think a ghost killed Vincent?" Katie whispered.

Before Maddie could answer, she was interrupted by Barbara's voice drifting toward them.

"Richard, I'm not going anywhere. If we take off now, we'll lose everything." Barbara's stern tone filled the kitchen. "You just need to keep it together. No one knows anything."

"That's not true. Is it, Maddie?" Richard suddenly looked straight at the doorway of the kitchen where Maddie and Katie were just barely hidden by shadows.

Maddie felt a rush of adrenalin. Were Richard and Barbara really the murderers? She knew she had only two choices. She could confront them and try to get a confession or pretend she knew nothing and let them disappear.

"I do know something." Maddie stepped into the kitchen.

Katie stepped in behind her.

Barbara and Richard watched Maddie as she cleared her throat, then continued.

"Barbara, you claimed it was your wedding dress I found. But I saw a picture of you in the dining room wearing a completely different dress on your wedding day, and we found a receipt for a wedding dress, and the date on the receipt was just a few weeks before Vincent died. A wig and makeup were also bought on the same day. That's when I worked out what really happened." Maddie settled her gaze on Barbara as Richard hovered beside her. "You knew that in order for your B&B to be successful, you'd have to get it lots of attention. So, you made up the legend of the Becket bride. Then, to make sure people believed it, you started dressing as her and scaring the locals when they came around to check on the new neighbors. I was one of those neighbors, and I've never forgotten seeing the Becket bride in the attic window."

"So, I decided to do some marketing. There's nothing wrong with that," Barbara said.

"Maybe not. But you lied to me about it. You lied to me about the dress. You lied to me about so many things. That made me wonder, why would you feel the need to lie?" Maddie took a step toward her. "It's because you can't have anyone looking too closely at your past. You can't have anyone knowing that you're the reason Vincent died."

"Watch your mouth," Richard roared. The once placid man shifted into an intimidating force as he stalked toward Maddie. "You don't stand under our roof and accuse my wife like that."

"Don't act as if you don't know about it, Richard. It won't save you." Maddie willed herself not to take a step back. Jake's advice to find a weapon to protect herself with now made perfect sense. Too bad she hadn't taken it. She'd already confronted them, and their reactions made her certain her assumption was right. But now she faced two murderers and their desperation to keep their secret.

"Stop, Richard! Don't you say another word!" Barbara stepped between him and Maddie. "She's trying to trick us. She wants us to say something that will make us look guilty so that she can run the kids out of business. Are you going to try to take over Becket House? Has that been your plan this whole time? Maybe that's why you killed Adam!"

"She had nothing to do with Adam's murder!" Katie stepped forward, a few inches closer to Barbara.

In one sharp movement, Barbara grabbed her around the neck and shoulders with one arm and pulled her back against her chest. In the other hand, she revealed a kitchen knife, which she held close to Katie's side.

CHAPTER 26

"*D*on't!" Maddie's stomach lurched, and her mind spun with dizziness and panic as she looked at the knife. "Please! Don't hurt her, Barbara! Just let her go!"

Katie squeezed her eyes shut and stood very still.

"I don't want to hurt anyone. I never did." Barbara sighed, but kept her grip tight on Katie.

"I know what happened with Vincent." Maddie wanted to keep her talking. Maybe as time passed, they would calm down and realize they didn't want to hurt anyone else. "The Becket bride was on the roof with him. But she wasn't a ghost. It was you."

"Very clever." Barbara nodded. "When Vincent found out about our plan to make up a ghost story to set up the house as a haunted B&B, he didn't want to. He didn't believe in ghosts. So, I told him he could forget about being part of the business and just move on with his life. But he refused. He kept insisting he owned part of the business, and he wouldn't allow us to con people. He even said he would go to the police. I doubt they would have done anything, but I wanted the business to be successful, and I thought making it a haunted B&B would be the best way to do that. So, I thought the best solution would be to convince him it was a true story."

"So, you dressed as the ghost of the bride?" Maddie tried to keep her voice even and work out how she was going to get Katie out of this.

"Yes, that's when I got the dress, the wig, and the makeup. I waited until I knew Vincent would be here alone. I lured him into the attic with thumps and scratching. When he saw me, he got so scared, he ran out onto the roof." Barbara paused as tears filled her eyes. "I went after him, to stop him, to save him. But that's not what he saw. He didn't see me, he saw the Becket bride chasing after him. He slipped and fell off the roof." She sniffled. "Don't you see? I never meant for him to die. It was an accident! I didn't kill him!"

"Maybe you didn't push him, but you caused him to die and covered it up," Maddie said.

"I did what I had to do." Barbara tightened her grip on Katie.

"Let me go, please!" Katie wriggled in her grasp.

"Don't you move a muscle." Richard scowled at Katie.

"Everything's fake. The silhouettes we've been seeing, the lights flickering, the crashes, everything?" Maddie wanted to keep them talking. Maybe she could buy some time and get them to release Katie.

"Yes. Things could have stayed the same. No one would be any the wiser about the fake effects." Richard stomped his foot against the floor. "But Cynthia and Dirk agreed to do the documentary, and it was too late. They wouldn't listen to us. They knew about the fake effects to make the place look haunted, but they didn't know what happened to Vincent. They presumed he just fell off the roof, and people made up the stories of the bride being up there because they knew about the stories of the ghost. They had no idea Barbara was really up there dressed as the bride."

"But Adam suspected something was up, and he wanted to find out the truth. He was asking too many questions, and that's why Cynthia contacted a lawyer to try and get out of the deal? She didn't want the fact that they were using fake effects to be revealed?" Maddie suggested.

"Yes. If Adam hadn't gone digging, none of this would have happened. I didn't even realize we still had the receipts. When Adam came to me with them, I knew then that he had already discovered too much. So, I gave him the opportunity to join in on the lie with us. At the very least, he would reveal that we were using special effects to make the B&B seem haunted. The business would have been ruined. But there were witnesses who saw the ghost of the bride when Vincent fell. I knew if he told the truth about the Becket bride being a hoax, it would place Barbara in the attic at the time that Vincent died, and our whole lives would change forever." Richard glanced at Barbara. "Our lives would be ruined."

"Not to mention the lives of Dirk and Cynthia," Barbara said.

"I offered Adam money, but he refused." Richard shook his head. "He said the scandal would make a better story than just a haunted house. When I went out into the rain to speak to him again about it, he'd found our old lights and projectors we used to fool guests. Cynthia and Dirk had just replaced them with more modern equipment. They tossed the old stuff out in the back until they could get rid of it properly. They presumed no one would ever find them there, and if they did, they wouldn't know what they were for. But Adam found them. He wouldn't listen to reason. We had to protect our reputation and the business."

"Did Cynthia and Dirk have anything to do with his murder?" Maddie could see the desperation in Katie's eyes.

"No, we took care of everything. We had no choice. Adam left us no choice." Barbara shook her head. "When he reached down to get his phone out of the water, I hit him on the back of the head with a sandbag. Then I held him down. When I turned him over and saw he was actually dead, I couldn't believe I'd killed him. But I did."

"We both did it. We did it together, Barbara," Richard said.

"We did." Barbara turned an adoring gaze on him. "And now we have to take care of this problem."

CHAPTER 27

"*W*ait, please." Maddie inched closer as she kept her eyes trained on the knife pressed against Katie's side. "You didn't have a choice then, but you do have a choice now. Vincent's death was an accident. As far as anyone knows, Adam's death could have also been an accident. You don't have to do this. You can let Katie go, let all of us go, and go on with your life."

"That's not possible, my dear." Richard shook his head. "You've been communicating with the chief of police this whole time. We'd just been discussing getting into our boat and taking off, and we would have, if you hadn't shown up. Now our plans have changed. We need to clean this up and make it nice and tidy." He raised his eyebrows. "Don't we, Barbara?"

"Yes, we do, dear." Barbara smiled warmly at him.

"But how?" Maddie gasped. "We're not the only people here. Everyone is going to be looking for us. You can't kill all of us!"

"Oh, but we can. You see, there's a basement." Barbara kept Katie held tight in her arms. "It's full of water right now. So full, that if people were trapped down there, they wouldn't survive. Can you imagine the stories they'll tell? An entire group of people tragically drowned on Halloween night, murdered by the ghosts that haunt the house. The police will presume it was an accident, and they will find your confessions to murdering Adam. But we'll spin a story about ghosts to the public. People will line up for miles to stay here, and Dirk and Cynthia will be set up for life. So trust me, there's no benefit to me keeping any of you alive."

"You would really do that?" Katie cleared her throat. "You'd murder nine more people? Aren't the two you've already murdered enough?"

"I didn't murder Vincent," Barbara snapped as she continued to hold on to Katie. "It wasn't my fault. It was an accident. We knew Vincent was a real honest guy. He didn't like to lie or play games. He just wanted to always be right. Of course, that's not the way a business runs. He questioned everything about the story of the Becket bride." She rolled her eyes. "I didn't kill him, but he paid the price for his stubbornness, and so will you."

"Just stop this now." Maddie reached for Katie's hand. "Let her come with me, and we'll never say a word about it. Please!"

"No!" Richard opened the door to the basement. "If you don't get down there, I'll make sure she doesn't make it to the basement in the first place."

Maddie's muscles tightened with fear as she watched Barbara pull Katie toward the basement door.

"Jake's on his way here." Maddie blurted the words out without thinking them through. "He's on his way, and he'll be here before you can get rid of us. This is your last chance to get out before he shows up and arrests you both!"

"Yeah, right, like he's going to get here in this storm." Barbara sneered. "There's no chance any cops are coming near this place until the weather clears."

"You're wrong!" Maddie tried to fill her voice with confidence. "Jake isn't just a friend of mine.

We're in love, and he'll stop at nothing to make sure I'm safe. He's already sent me a text that he's found a way here. So, do you want to waste your time killing us one by one, or do you want to make your getaway while you still can?"

"See, Barbara! I told you we should have just gotten on the boat. We would have been long gone before they would have realized what we'd done, and Cynthia and Dirk would have been fine." Richard jerked his thumb toward the basement door. "Toss her down there and let's go."

Barbara shoved Katie toward the open basement door.

Katie let out a scream as she stumbled forward and tripped over the first step.

Richard and Barbara ran toward the back door off the kitchen and quickly disappeared into the rain.

Maddie lunged toward the basement as she heard a splash in the darkness.

"Katie!" Maddie shrieked as she clung to the railing of the staircase with one hand and shined the flashlight from her phone with her other hand.

"Katie?" Tammy ran into the kitchen, her voice filled with fear. "Did I hear Katie scream?"

"It's okay, I've got her, Tammy. I've got her."

Maddie eased Katie up out of the water as she coughed and sputtered. "She's okay. Right, sweetheart?"

"I'm okay." Katie continued to cough as she climbed the stairs. She hugged her mother.

"Is Jake really coming, Maddie?" Katie looked over at her.

"No, I made all of that up. There's no way he's going to get here in this storm. But we have to get everyone together and find a way out of here. As long as Richard and Barbara are on the loose, they're a threat. I'm sure if they can't get away, they'll come back for us." Maddie locked eyes with Tammy. "Did you find Bella and Polly?"

"No, I'm so sorry." Tammy shook her head. "I looked everywhere for them. They must have gone back upstairs."

"All right, I'm going to find them. You get everyone together." Maddie looked over at Katie. "Are you sure you're okay?"

"I'm okay, Aunt Maddie. Thanks to you." Katie hugged her.

CHAPTER 28

*M*addie started on the third floor again as she searched for Bella and Polly. She needed to find them. As she started down toward the second floor, she suddenly heard a burst of barks.

"Downstairs!" Maddie gasped. "They're downstairs!" When she reached the second floor, she looked down the grand stairway to the first floor.

The water had reached the top of the bottom stair. She thought about running down the steps but felt as if it wouldn't be fast enough. Instead, she perched on the top of the railing and rode it down toward the bottom. As she slid faster than she expected, a cry of surprise escaped her lips. As if in reaction to her scream, all of the lights in the house went off again. She squinted through the darkness as a figure appeared at the bottom of the stairs.

It spread its arms as she reached the bottom of the railing and caught her easily.

"Jake!" Maddie gasped as she recognized him despite the darkness. "Bella and Polly! They're missing!"

"Don't worry, I already got them." Jake cradled her in his arms as he looked into her eyes. "They're safe. They're being taken to the boat with one of my men."

"They are? How?" Maddie felt immediate relief.

"I heard them barking when I came inside. I knew you'd want me to make sure they're safe. So, I handed them off to one of my men before I came looking for you." Jake smiled as he held her gaze. "And then you slid right into my arms."

"Oh, right." Maddie blushed as she began to squirm in his grasp. "You should probably put me down."

"And let you get your feet wet?" Jake's smile widened. "No, I'll carry you all the way to the boat."

"Don't you dare." Maddie's cheeks warmed. "Everyone will see."

"And?" Jake laughed. "What's so bad about that?"

"Put her down!" Amber shrieked from the top of the stairs.

Tammy pushed past her and ran straight down the stairs.

"Put her down, evil spirit." Tammy swung her hands against Jake's shoulders and chest.

"Okay, okay," Jake barked as he eased Maddie down to her feet. "Stop! Stop, now!" He caught Tammy's hands as they continued to pound his arms and chest.

"Stop, Tammy, it's Jake!" Maddie stepped between Jake and Tammy's hands, then turned to face Amber just as she was about to take a flying leap onto Jake. "Don't, Amber! It's Jake!"

"What?" Amber stumbled forward into Tammy.

"You're not a ghost?" Tammy pointed the flashlight on her phone at him.

"No, I'm not a ghost." The light revealed the stern expression on Jake's face. "Is there something you three want to tell me?"

"It's Richard and Barbara, Jake. They're the ones who killed Adam, and they killed Vincent, too. Well, they had a hand in it anyway. I think they probably took off on a boat when they realized you were here. You have to catch them." Maddie clung to his hand. "They're going to get away."

"Not a chance. The only reason I was able to get here is because I borrowed a high-powered boat from another town. They'll never get out of here with anything less." Jake pulled her close. "Now, let me get you all out of here."

In the blur of the next few hours, the rain stopped as everyone finally had the chance to leave Becket House. Within a few minutes, Richard and Barbara were caught. They'd wedged their boat between two trees and had nowhere to run. But it wasn't until Maddie set foot on her front porch with Bella and Polly beside her that she felt genuine relief. She let the dogs run into the house, then turned back to face Jake, who had walked her to the door.

"Can I come in for a cupcake?" Jake asked.

"I happen to have a few stashed inside." Maddie smiled at the thought. "And I'll make you a coffee."

"Great. I need something sweet after such a rough Halloween."

"I know you've been through a lot. I can only imagine how hard it was dealing with the chaos of Halloween, plus fielding my calls and texts the whole time."

"That's not why it was rough." Jake followed behind her into the house.

The dogs bolted past both of their legs, eager to get to their fluffy, warm beds.

"It's not?" Maddie continued into the kitchen. She gave the dogs fresh water and put on the coffeepot. She got a couple of cupcakes from the fridge, then turned around and offered him one. "To get you started, while you wait for the coffee."

"Thank you." Jake's smile grew wide. "I'm just so glad you're okay. It was a rough night because of knowing you were in danger and not being able to protect you. It was terrible."

"But I'm okay." Maddie smiled. "I made it out all right, didn't I?"

"Yes. You did." Jake kissed her cheek. "You're amazing. You'll have to tell me exactly how you got Richard and Barbara to let you go."

Maddie recalled the lie she'd told them that made them release Katie. At least she'd thought it was a lie. But it had actually been the truth. Jake was on his way to save her, even when she had no idea he was. Was that the only part of her lie that had turned out to be true? Or did she and Jake really love each other? It sure seemed as if he would do absolutely anything to get to her. She slid her arms around his neck and looked into his eyes.

"Thank you, Jake, for trusting me to help figure all of this out and for always coming to my rescue."

"I always will." Jake grinned as he swept her up into his arms. "Now that no one's watching, I can carry you wherever I want."

"Jake!" Maddie laughed.

The End

MADDIE'S CINNAMON CUPCAKE RECIPE

Ingredients:

Cupcakes:

1 1/4 cups all-purpose flour

3/4 teaspoon baking powder

1/4 teaspoon baking soda

1/2 teaspoon salt

2 teaspoons ground cinnamon

1/2 cup (1 stick) unsalted butter, softened to room temperature

1/2 cup superfine sugar

1/2 cup light brown sugar

2 large eggs, at room temperature

1/4 cup vegetable oil
1 teaspoon vanilla extract
3/4 cup buttermilk, at room temperature

Cinnamon Buttercream Frosting:

2 sticks (1 cup) unsalted butter, softened to room
temperature
3 to 3 1/2 cups confectioners' sugar
1 to 2 tablespoons milk
1 teaspoon vanilla extract
1 teaspoon ground cinnamon
1/4 teaspoon salt

Optional: Gel food coloring to color the frosting.
Halloween cupcake toppers for decoration.

Preparation:

Preheat the oven to 350 degrees Fahrenheit.

Line the muffin pans with paper cupcake liners.
This recipe makes 12 cupcakes.

Sift the flour, baking powder, baking soda, salt, and
cinnamon into a bowl.

In another bowl, beat the butter until smooth. Then add the sugars and beat until light and fluffy.

Add the eggs, oil, and vanilla extract to the butter mixture and mix until combined.

Gradually add the buttermilk, alternating with the dry ingredients. Mix until combined.

Divide between the cupcake liners.

Bake for 16 to 20 minutes until a skewer inserted into the middle comes out clean.

Leave to cool in the pan for about 10 minutes, then transfer to a wire rack to cool completely.

To prepare the cinnamon buttercream frosting, beat the butter until smooth.

Add 3 cups of confectioners' sugar, 1 tablespoon of milk, vanilla extract, cinnamon, and salt. Beat until well-combined and fluffy. To get the desired consistency, gradually add more milk if too thick or add more confectioners' sugar if too thin. Mix in a few drops of the food coloring if desired.

Spoon or pipe the frosting on top of the cupcakes.

Decorate with Halloween-themed cupcake toppers.

Enjoy!!

ABOUT THE AUTHOR

Cindy Bell is a USA Today and Wall Street Journal Bestselling Author. She is the author of the Little Leaf Creek, Wagging Tail, Donut Truck, Dune House, Sage Gardens, Chocolate Centered, Macaron Patisserie, Nuts about Nuts, Bekki the Beautician, Heavenly Highland Inn and Wendy the Wedding Planner cozy mystery series.

Cindy has always loved reading, but it is only recently that she has discovered her passion for writing romantic cozy mysteries. She loves walking along the beach thinking of the next adventure her characters can embark on.

You can sign up for her newsletter so you are notified of her latest releases at http://www. cindybellbooks.com.

ALSO BY CINDY BELL

MADDIE MILLS COZY MYSTERIES

DUNE HOUSE COZY MYSTERIES

9 - 12)

Dune House Cozy Mystery Series Boxed Set 4 (Books 13 - 16)

Seaside Secrets

Boats and Bad Guys

Treasured History

Hidden Hideaways

Dodgy Dealings

Suspects and Surprises

Ruffled Feathers

A Fishy Discovery

Danger in the Depths

Celebrities and Chaos

Pups, Pilots and Peril

Tides, Trails and Trouble

Racing and Robberies

Athletes and Alibis

Manuscripts and Deadly Motives

Pelicans, Pier and Poison

Sand, Sea and a Skeleton

Pianos and Prison

Relaxation, Reunions and Revenge

A Tangled Murder

Fame, Food and Murder

Beaches and Betrayal

Fatal Festivities

Sunsets, Smoke and Suspicion

Hobbies and Homicide

Anchors and Abduction

Friends, Family and Fugitives

LITTLE LEAF CREEK COZY MYSTERIES

Little Leaf Creek Cozy Mystery Series 10 Book Box Set
(Books 1-10)

Little Leaf Creek Cozy Mystery Series Box Set Vol 1
(Books 1-3)

Little Leaf Creek Cozy Mystery Series Box Set Vol 2
(Books 3-6)

Little Leaf Creek Cozy Mystery Series Box Set Vol 3
(Books 7-9)

Little Leaf Creek Cozy Mystery Series Box Set Vol 4
(Books 10-12)

Little Leaf Creek Cozy Mystery Series Box Set Vol 5
(Books 13-15)

Chaos in Little Leaf Creek

CHOCOLATE CENTERED COZY MYSTERIES

Cherries, Berries and a Body

Christmas Cookies and Criminals

Grapes, Ganache & Guilt

Yule Logs & Murder

Mocha, Marriage and Murder

Holiday Fudge and Homicide

Chocolate Mousse and Murder

SAGE GARDENS COZY MYSTERIES

Sage Gardens Cozy Mystery 10 Book Box Set (Books 1 - 10)

Sage Gardens Cozy Mystery Series Box Set Volume 1 (Books 1 - 4)

Sage Gardens Cozy Mystery Series Box Set Volume 2 (Books 5 - 8)

Birthdays Can Be Deadly

Money Can Be Deadly

Trust Can Be Deadly

Ties Can Be Deadly

Rocks Can Be Deadly

Jewelry Can Be Deadly

Numbers Can Be Deadly

DONUT TRUCK COZY MYSTERIES

WAGGING TAIL COZY MYSTERIES

NUTS ABOUT NUTS COZY MYSTERIES

BEKKI THE BEAUTICIAN COZY MYSTERIES

Hairspray and Homicide

A Dyed Blonde and a Dead Body

Mascara and Murder

Pageant and Poison

Conditioner and a Corpse

Mistletoe, Makeup and Murder

Hairpin, Hair Dryer and Homicide

Blush, a Bride and a Body

Shampoo and a Stiff

Cosmetics, a Cruise and a Killer

Lipstick, a Long Iron and Lifeless

Camping, Concealer and Criminals

Treated and Dyed

A Wrinkle-Free Murder

A MACARON PATISSERIE COZY MYSTERY

Sifting for Suspects

Recipes and Revenge

Mansions, Macarons and Murder

HEAVENLY HIGHLAND INN COZY MYSTERIES

WENDY THE WEDDING PLANNER COZY MYSTERIES

Made in the USA
Coppell, TX
15 November 2023

24291638R00125